"Did you ever choice?"

"We chose each other, Laura. Our feelings for each other had nothing to do with my background. That hasn't changed."

"Everything's changed."

"Because my past is different than you thought?"

"Because my future is different. Our son's future is different."

This morning, when she'd awakened, her life had been everything she'd ever wanted. She had a thriving business. She thought she was married to the man of her dreams. And she had a perfect little son on the way.

And now her marriage—everything she knew—was gone.

ANN VOSS PETERSON

MARITAL PRIVILEGE

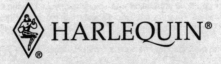

HARLEQUIN®

TORONTO • NEW YORK • LONDON
AMSTERDAM • PARIS • SYDNEY • HAMBURG
STOCKHOLM • ATHENS • TOKYO • MILAN • MADRID
PRAGUE • WARSAW • BUDAPEST • AUCKLAND

Special thanks to Lynda Sandoval, Linda Style,
Susan Vaughan and Virginia Kelly for their help
filling the gaps in my limited knowledge.
To my critique partners Carol Voss and Judith Lyons.
And to my family for doing without wife and mother
while I battled the Russian mob.

ISBN 0-373-22878-3

MARITAL PRIVILEGE

Copyright © 2005 by Ann Voss Peterson

www.eHarlequin.com

Printed in U.S.A.

ABOUT THE AUTHOR

Ever since she was a little girl making her own books out of construction paper, Ann Voss Peterson wanted to write. So when it came time to choose a major at the University of Wisconsin, creative writing was her only choice. Of course, writing wasn't a *practical* choice—one needs to earn a living. So Ann found jobs ranging from proofreading legal transcripts, to working with quarter horses, to washing windows. But no matter how she earned her paycheck, she continued to write the type of stories that captured her heart and imagination—romantic suspense. Ann lives near Madison, Wisconsin, with her husband, her two young sons, her Border collie and her quarter horse mare. Ann loves to hear from readers. E-mail her at ann@annvosspeterson.com or visit her Web site at annvosspeterson.com.

Books by Ann Voss Peterson

CAST OF CHARACTERS

Alec Martin—Born Nikolai Stanislov, Alec has tried to build a new life since entering the Witness Security Program. But when the man he sent to prison—his own father—is paroled, he has to run to save his life—and that of his wife and unborn son.

Laura Martin—She thought she was married to the man of her dreams, a safe caring man, only to find out he's the son of a mobster. But before she can figure out if she still has a marriage, she has to run for her life.

Ivan Stanislov—The powerful head of a faction of the Russian Mafiya, Ivan wants revenge almost as much as he wants his unborn grandson.

Wayne Bigelow—The reporter says he wants to help Alec. Can he be trusted?

Tony Griggs—When the U.S. Marshal died, he gave away Alec's new identity. Now his murder might bring Ivan Stanislov down.

Detective Mylinski—Is the seemingly honest cop beyond suspicion?

Special Agent Callahan—He needs Alec's help to bring down Ivan Stanislov, but will he be able to honor his promise to keep Alec safe?

Sergei Kamarov—The murderous brute wants revenge and to regain his place in the warm spot.

Pavel Tverdovsky—The young thug is the future of the Russian mob.

Chapter One

Alec Martin stared at the photo of U.S. Marshal Tony Griggs on the morning news and struggled to wrap his mind around what he was seeing. He stepped toward the television set suspended high above the scarred oak bar. "Can we turn up the sound?"

The bartender glanced up from his cup of morning coffee and the list of booze he needed to order. "No remote. Lost it during a Packer game a couple years ago. You want to climb on the bar and turn it up? Hey? Be my guest."

Alec didn't move. The stiff collar of his dress shirt choked him. Sweat slicked his palms. He'd dreaded this day for ten long years. Even now he didn't want to believe what he was seeing.

Snips of headlines scrolling under the talking head, CNN style.

Retired U.S. marshal killed.

Signs of torture found.

The screen focused on a balding police detective named Mylinski. Frustration knotted Alec's aching gut. He had to know more, and staring at a soundless interview with a tight-lipped cop wasn't doing a damn bit of good. He grasped his cell phone from his belt and flipped it open. Spinning on his heel, he made for the door, punching in Wayne's direct number at the *Brooklyn Chronicle* from memory.

"I haven't given you my liquor order yet," the bartender's annoyed Wisconsin accent sounded from the bar.

"I have to make a call," Alec shouted over his shoulder as he pushed outside. The morning sunlight blinded him for a minute, but he didn't slow his pace.

The secretary answered on the second ring. *"Brooklyn Chronicle."*

Alec didn't recognize her voice. "Wayne Bigelow, please."

"I'm sorry, Mr. Bigelow is in a meeting. Would you like his voice mail?"

"No." The last thing Alec was going to do was leave him a message. Not about this. "Interrupt the meeting."

"Excuse me?"

"Do it. This is an emergency."

"That may be, Mr...."

"Stanislov." Alec never thought he'd hear the name come from his lips again. It rested on his tongue like a curse word, bitter, cruel. "Nika Stanislov."

"I'm sorry, Mr. Stanislov, but I'm not going to interrupt an important meeting for—"

"Tell him the name."

"Excuse me?"

"Tell Bigelow the name. Nika Stanislov. He'll take my call."

"Please hold," she said, her exasperation coming across loud and clear. A click sounded, and canned music took over the line.

Alec strode across the parking lot, pulse hammering louder than the drone of synthesized strings in his ear. If anyone would know what was going on, it was Bigelow. He'd better, anyway. With Griggs gone, Alec sure as hell didn't trust anyone in law enforcement.

He dipped his free hand in his pocket, pulled out his SUV's keyless remote and unlocked the vehicle before he reached it. He shrugged out of his suit jacket and threw it inside. His ass had just hit the driver's seat when Bigelow's voice boomed over the phone.

"Nika. My God, how are you?"

"Is he out?"

"Yesterday."

The knot tightened. Alec had always thought he'd know the day the bastard got out of prison. That he'd feel the vibration in the air. Smell the stench. Something. But he hadn't had a clue.

"I would have called, but…" Bigelow let his sentence trail off. There was no point finishing.

"Yeah, I know." Bigelow didn't know where Alec was. Nobody knew where Alec was. At least, no one was supposed to.

"Didn't the Marshals' Service tell you he was up for early parole?"

"No."

"Probably a screw-up between state and feds. Typical."

Alec wished this was a typical screw-up. But his gut told him different. "Griggs is dead."

"Griggs?"

"A U.S. marshal on my case. The one in charge of relocating me."

"When?"

"I just saw it on the news. Breaking story from Madison."

"Madison?"

"Wisconsin."

Bigelow let loose a string of curses. "Doesn't anyone around here stay up on the news? We'd better have a reporter on a flight to Wisconsin right now, or someone's going to lose his head."

Alec turned the key in the ignition. The SUV roared to life.

"Where are you, Nika?"

"I'd rather not say."

"You want me to call the cops for you?"

"No cops."

"FBI? I know a guy—"

"No."

"What are you going to do?"

"Whatever I have to." And the first thing on his list was finding Laura. Now. "I've got to go."

"Will I hear from you again?"

"I don't know."

"Let me give you my cell."

As soon as he finished reciting the number, Alec cut off the call. He had to reach Laura. And he was afraid he didn't have a second to lose.

He hit her number on his cell's speed dial. His wife's phone service picked up on the second ring. A pleasant voice directed him to her voice mail. Damn. Laura was always forgetting to turn on her cell phone. And at this hour in the morning, the restaurant's answering machine would still be on.

He ended the call without leaving a message, and concentrated on driving. He had to get to the restaurant. He had to reach Laura. If Griggs had been tortured, he could have caved. He could have spilled Alec's location. And if that happened, dear old Dad and his thugs were already on their way.

Pushing the accelerator to the floor, he raced down streets and around curves until he reached the strip mall at the edge of the tiny-but-growing town of Beaver Falls. Nestled at the end of the mall next to the Cup-N-Sup coffee shop and a women's clothing store sat Laura's pride and joy, The Blue Ox Café. The parking lot in front was still empty. It wouldn't get busy until eleven o'clock, when Laura threw open the door for the lunch crowd.

Tires squealing their protest, Alec gunned the SUV around the building to the back lot. Three cars dotted the employee parking area. Laura's blue van was not among them, but he spotted her partner's Jeep. She'd probably hitched a ride with Sally, as she often did. He could only hope that was the case. If today was errand day, he might not be able to reach her for hours. And by then it might be too late.

He stopped the SUV at the curb behind a produce truck and jumped out. Dodging a ripe-smelling Dumpster, he dashed to the employee entrance and ducked inside.

No sound came from the kitchen, not the rattle of pans on the cook's line, not the slam of the walk-in cooler's door as the produce guy made his delivery. Heart knocking against his rib cage, Alec stepped into the kitchen. His shoes squeaked on rubber mats stretched over red tile. He moved as quietly as possible, walking through the prep kitchen, peeking into the deserted line. The odor of deep fryers hung in the air, heavy as an approaching storm. And there was something else. Another odor. Familiar but too faint for him to identify.

Pulse pounding in his ears, he ducked back into the prep kitchen. Next to a slab of prime rib, a meat cleaver lay on a cutting board, blood dulling the shine of its razor-sharp edge. He grasped the wood handle. Weapon poised in front of him, he stepped into the waiters' aisle that led into the dining room.

Music drifted from the dining room, the high-pitched tone of strings rasping his nerves like cheese across a grater. The scent grew stronger.

Natural gas.

The restaurant was filled with it. Flammable. Highly explosive. He had to do something. If he didn't, it wouldn't take long for gas to reach the flames heating deep fryers and ovens on the cook's line.

He spun around and raced through the waiters' aisle and into the kitchen, his shoes squeaking on the mats. Reaching the cook's line, he switched off fryers and ovens. He extinguished each pilot light and turned off every gas valve he could spot. It wouldn't be enough. The leak hadn't originated in the kitchen. The scent was strongest in the dining room. Even if by some miracle he found the leak, there was enough gas already hanging in the air to blow the place. All that was missing was a flame. But it wouldn't be missing for long. Once the furnace clicked on, the gas would ignite. It would be all over. If anyone was in the building, he had to get them out. He had to find Laura.

And as much as he didn't trust the police, he needed help. He flipped open his cell phone and punched in the number.

"Nine-one-one," a woman's voice answered.

"There's a gas leak at the Blue Ox Café."

"What is your name, sir?"

Alec hesitated. "That's not important. There's something else going on, too. I'm not sure what, but the place seems deserted. You've got to get the police out here. Hurry." He cut off the call. Clipping his cell phone back on his belt, he clutched the meat cleaver, rounded the corner of the waiters' aisle and stepped into the dining room.

As he rounded the corner, another odor hit him. A sweet copper scent that mixed with the natural gas and turned his stomach. He slowed his pace, weaving through tables, listening for anything out of the ordinary. He circled a row of booths and inched across the open center of the dining room, and jolted to a stop.

Dark blotches fouled the multicolored carpet and streaked a table in the center of the room. And beyond the table—

"Oh my God." Cleaver in front of him, Alec raced toward the bodies, waiting for a flash of movement, a gun to his head, a blade between his ribs.

He reached Laura's prep cook first. His chef's whites were black with blood from the slash across his throat. His eyes stared blankly at the ceiling.

There was no helping him. No saving him. Cursing his father, Alec moved on to the next body.

A waitress no older than twenty curled around a table leg at the edge of the dining room, as if she'd been hiding when the bullet had drilled into her chest and stolen her life. Her face was swollen, purple with bruises. She'd taken a beating before the bullet. And that pointed to one man. A sadistic bastard who got his kicks beating women before he killed them. His father's right-hand thug, Sergei Komorov.

Gritting his teeth, Alec left the waitress and

moved to the final prone form. The middle-aged guy who delivered produce had made it as far as the tile floor in front of the hostess stand before he'd been shot. His blood puddled under him and ran in rivers between the tiles.

Panic roared in Alec's ears. The odors of blood and gas clogged his throat. Three dead. Where the hell was Laura?

There was one place left. He straightened from beside the produce guy's body and forced his feet to move. Laura and Sally usually opened the kitchen first thing in the morning. By this time, they had moved to the bar.

He raced into the lounge. The room was cloaked in shadow, heavy wood blinds drawn over the windows. He led with the meat cleaver, checking behind half walls and plants, glancing under the row of bar stools. No blood. No bodies.

No Laura.

Relieved, he tried to block the image of his beautiful wife bloodied, dead. He had to find her. She had to be okay. Laura was his life, his future.

Laura and their unborn son.

He stepped behind the bar. Booze bottles that spent the night under lock and key lined the rail. The till was open, its tray of cash not yet in place. Someone had been opening the bar when this had happened.

Alec tried to breathe, tried to stay calm. He strode over the rubber mats, straight for the closed office door at the end of the bar.

Dread blared in his ears like a siren. He closed his fingers around the cool brass doorknob. Turning it, he yanked the door open.

A body leaned back in the chair. Long blond hair streaked dark with blood. A plastic tie clasped feminine hands together at the wrists. Broken and battered, fingers jutted at strange angles.

A sob shook from his chest. He grasped the back of the chair with trembling hands. Holding his breath, he spun it around. Blood coagulated, sticky beneath a slashed throat. Her face was so bruised and swollen, it was almost unrecognizable. She stared at him through blue eyes glazed with death.

Blue eyes.

Another sob tore from his gut. *Sally, not Laura.*

He averted his eyes from her face, ashamed at the relief welling within him. Spilling over. Sally, not Laura. Laura might still be alive.

But where was she?

If Laura had left to run errands, there might be a clue as to where she went, what the restaurant needed. He studied the desk. Blood spattered the surface, the three-ring binders, the papers detailing the Blue Ox's liquor order—the order he was to pick up later that morning. He raised his eyes to the computer screen. A pink message slip stuck to one side of the screen, a simple message scrawled on the front.

"Laura sick. Won't be in until late. Sally, could you open bar?"

Cold dread throbbed in Alec's ears and pumped through his veins. He had to get home. He only prayed he wasn't too late. Because if he had spotted the message, he could be sure his father and his men had spotted it, too.

And they'd already be on their way.

Chapter Two

Alec raced into the restaurant's entryway. The odor of gas had grown stronger. It now completely choked out the coppery scent of blood. Any second now it would hit the furnace flame, and the whole place would go up. He couldn't do anything more here. He had to get out.

Instead of retracing his steps to the back kitchen entrance, he raced for the closed front door. He twisted the dead bolt and threw the door open.

Fresh air hit him in the face like a splash of cool water. He launched into a run, sprinting down the sidewalk toward the parking lot.

Movement caught his eye. A woman stepped out of the Cup-N-Sup, steaming coffee in hand.

Oh, hell.

He veered for the coffee shop. "Get out of here. There's a gas leak next door."

The woman's eyes widened. Clutching her cup, she ran for her car.

He dove for the coffee shop's door and yanked it open. "Everyone needs to evacuate."

Two employees and half a dozen customers turned to stare at him. None made a move.

"There's a gas leak next door. The building is going to blow. You need to get out."

Several customers shot for the door. Others narrowed their eyes, as if trying to figure out what he was up to.

He glanced out the coffee shop's window, willing flashing red and blue lights to appear on the street outside, a siren to pierce the air. Where the hell were the police?

He turned his attention back to the skeptical people in front of him, raking his mind for something to make them move before it was too late. "It's a terrorist attack. Get out."

They headed for the door in a wave.

He followed. "Get as far from the building as you can. Run."

People scattered.

Alec moved to the clothing store. After shooing the owner and a customer out, he circled to the parking lot in the rear of the building where he'd left his SUV. He needed to get home to Laura. To get her out before his father and his men found their house.

Please God, don't let me be too late.

He cleared the hedge surrounding the rear parking lot. Feet hitting pavement, he raced for the SUV.

A rumble caught his ear. A thundering boom hit him in the chest, followed by the whoosh of sucking air. The ground shook. Sound exploded. He dove back behind the hedge. Flattening his body to the ground, he covered his head with his arms. Heat seared him. Debris hit him, cutting his arms, striking his back. The taste of blood flooded his mouth.

He raised his head, peering over the hedge. A ball of flame enveloped the building. His SUV stood silhouetted against the inferno, it and the produce truck reduced to nothing but twisted and blackened heaps of steel.

Hell.

He forced himself to his feet, trying to draw breath. His lungs seized and burned. There wasn't enough oxygen. Wasn't enough air. He stumbled toward the street. He had to find someone to take him home. He had to reach Laura before it was too late.

The street looked as solid as a jammed parking lot, drivers gaping at the ball of fire where a strip mall used to be.

He forced his legs to carry him over the curb,

across the asphalt to the cars. The first driver hit
the gas when she saw him and raced past wide-
eyed. A man driving a panel truck rolled down the
window. "Hey, buddy. You need an ambulance?"
He pulled out a cell phone and punched 911.

Alec leaned on the hood to steady himself. "I
need you to take me to my house. Please."

"From the look of ya, an ambulance is a better idea."

Alec looked down at himself. His white dress
shirt was tattered. Blood soaked through the right
sleeve. His tie hung like a cut noose around his
neck. No wonder the first driver had hit the gas
when she'd seen him coming. No wonder this
guy wanted to strap him to a stretcher. But it
didn't matter. Reaching Laura was the only thing
that mattered. "You don't understand. The men
who did this, they're after my wife. I have to get
home."

The guy held up a finger. "This will just take
a minute, pal. Hold on. The police and ambulance will give you the help you need."

Fat chance. The police should have been here
already.

A chill swept over Alec. His father had wide-
reaching power. Enough power to keep news of
his pending prison release from reaching Alec.
Enough power to kill a U.S. marshal. Did he have

enough power to delay the police in Beaver Falls? Did his money and muscle reach all the way to small-town Wisconsin?

Alec turned away and ran back across the street toward the strip mall. On the edge of the sidewalk, several bicycles stood in a bike rack. He pulled out an unchained touring bike and swung a leg over the seat. Pain shot through his arm and back. He gritted his teeth. Settling on the seat, he pushed off, pedaling as fast as his legs would move.

The wind fanned the cuts and scrapes on his arms, drying the rivulets of blood. Pain burned along his nerves. His lungs screamed for air. He pushed on, piloting the bike along city streets and over hills until the brand-new housing development on the outskirts of town sprawled before him.

It was late April and the trees hadn't yet sprouted leaves. He could pick out his house among the many similar houses lining the gently curving streets. He could also pick out the dark-colored sedan parked at the curb a half block away in front of a home under construction. Just the kind of nondescript car his father always favored. And in the front seat was the unmistakable shadow of a man.

Alec's blood turned to ice.

He pumped the pedals harder, racing down the

hill. Negotiating streets he knew well, he passed his street and turned up the cul-de-sac backing up to his house. He climbed off the bike and let it fall to the curb. Cutting through the neighbor's yard, he climbed over the low split-rail fence separating the backyards.

Hunkering down in a copse of trees and bushes, he surveyed his house. Blinds were drawn over windows and patio door. There was no sign of movement. Nothing unusual. Nothing, that is, but the hum of Alec's nerves.

They were inside. He could feel it.

He scooped in a deep breath. What could he do? How could he fight them? How could he get Laura out of there?

He'd never owned a gun. After escaping his father's world, he couldn't stand the thought of owning a weapon of violence. At the moment his protest seemed stupid, naive. What he wouldn't give to have a gun in his hand right now.

He crept around the edge of the yard, running half-crouched. Reaching the garage, he sidled between the fence and the wall until he drew even with a window barely large enough for a man to slip through. With any luck, his father and his thugs hadn't thought of anyone coming through the garage. They'd be focused on the street in front.

And on Laura.

He pushed horrible images from his mind. He couldn't let himself imagine what Sergei Komorov might be doing to his wife—what the bastard might have already done while Alec had been discovering the bodies in the restaurant and evacuating people from the strip mall. Laura had to be all right. If Sergei had touched her, Alec would strangle him with his bare hands.

He punched his fingers through the screen, the nylon ripping with ease. Grasping the bottom edge of the screen's frame, he pulled it up and pried it from the window. Now he just had the window itself. He couldn't break it, couldn't risk the men inside hearing the glass shatter. Instead, he fitted his fingers to the seam between the upper and lower sash of the double-hung window and wiggled until the latch popped. Sliding the lower sash open, he unseated it then the upper and set them on the ground.

Funny how he'd made sure the windows in the rest of the house had double locks but he hadn't thought about the garage window. It had seemed too small to bother with, too separate from the rest of the house.

He could only hope the men inside hadn't thought of it, either.

He placed his hands on the window frame. Arm

throbbing, he hoisted his body through the little space and lowered himself inside until he stood on the lawnmower. So far, so good. Now for a weapon.

Stepping off the mower, he grabbed a shovel from a wall rack. He crept to the door leading to the kitchen and pressed his ear to the cool steel.

The rumble of male voices filtered through the door—voices colored with Russian flair and cut with a hard Brooklyn edge. Accents he'd hoped never to hear again.

Rage hardened in his gut. He gripped the shovel, knuckles white. He pressed his ear tighter to the door.

"What does Mr. Stanislov want done with her?" a voice he didn't recognize asked.

Laura. He was talking about Laura. She must still be alive. Relief sucked the strength from Alec's legs. He leaned on the door and strained to hear more.

"Ivan told me, bring back Nika." Sergei's voice boomed through the kitchen.

Alec's gut tightened. So dear old Dad hadn't made the trip. He'd sent his thugs to collect Alec. He was getting lazy in his old age.

"You going to take care of her, then? I know you like doing the women."

Sergei grunted. "I got to find out what Ivan wants us to do. I think he'll want the baby."

"You're not touching my son." Laura's voice chimed through the kitchen strong and clear.

Alec's heart clutched. Tears welled in his eyes. She sounded unhurt, unbowed.

And gloriously alive.

"Son? Ivan will like that. A grandson. Maybe the child will make up for the father."

"Grandson? What are you talking about? You have the wrong house. My name is Laura Martin, and I don't know anyone named Ivan."

"Ah, I see." Sergei's voice took on an amused lilt.

Guilt drilled deep into Alec's chest. He should have told Laura the truth about who he really was from the beginning. He should have known he couldn't keep his past at bay forever.

He couldn't think about that right now. There would be time for regrets. Time for the truth to come out. Now he had to focus. Laura's and the baby's lives depended on it. The men inside would be armed with guns, and here he stood with nothing but a shovel. He had to even the odds, give himself a fighting chance.

He fingered his cell phone with his free hand. If he could distract at least one of the men, make sure he was out of the kitchen, away from Laura, maybe he could surprise the other before the thug could draw his gun.

Alec unclipped his phone from his belt and entered his home phone number from the speed dial directory.

Inside the kitchen he could hear the phone ring.

He pushed his ear to the door.

"I should get that." Laura's voice. "It's probably Sally from the restaurant. If I don't answer, she'll send someone over. Probably the police."

"She will not be sending anyone," Sergei growled.

"You don't know her. She worries about me like she's my mother."

"She's dead. Slit her throat myself."

Laura gasped.

Alec gripped on the shovel with sweat-slick hands, the image of Sally's battered and lifeless body sharp in his mind's eye.

Sergei's guttural laugh filtered through the door. "Don't worry. As soon as the baby comes, you'll be joining her. Unless I get impatient and cut him out of your belly."

Alec gritted his teeth. It was all he could do to stay where he was. To wait. The bastard wasn't going to touch his wife, or their baby. He'd see to it.

The phone continued to ring. Finally the answering machine picked up. Moving silently away from the door, Alec ducked down behind Laura's van, set down the shovel, and cupped his mouth with one hand. When the answering machine's beep sounded, he talked into the phone in a low voice. "Look out the front window, you bastards. You might as well give up now." Alec snapped the phone shut and stuffed it into his pocket. He picked up the shovel and made for the door.

A single set of footsteps moved across the kitchen floor and thundered toward the front of the house.

Now was his chance. Shoving the door open, he burst into the kitchen swinging.

The shovel connected with Sergei's head before he could turn around. The sound of the blow echoed through the room. The force shuddered up Alec's arms.

Sergei bellowed like a mad bull. He staggered forward but didn't go down. Instead, he spun and reached for the gun in his waistband. He yanked it out and leveled it on Alec before he could land another blow.

Sergei fired. The shot went wide, the bullet ripping into the cabinetry beside Alec.

Alec swung the shovel again, this time connecting with Sergei's arm.

The brute cursed in Russian. The gun rattled to the floor.

Movement flashed in the corner of Alec's eye. Laura. But he didn't have time to turn his head before Sergei launched himself.

Alec swung, catching Sergei in the face with the shovel's sharp edge.

Blood slashed across his cheek and nose. He staggered back and fell against the cabinets.

Footsteps thundered from the front of the house.

Alec landed the shovel against Sergei's head again. He spun just in time to see the second man round the corner into the kitchen. The barrel of his gun stared Alec directly in the face.

A shot exploded in Alec's ears.

Chapter Three

Laura Martin lowered her bound hands and the Russian-made Makarov 9mm she'd managed to pick up from the floor. The weapon's report still echoed through the kitchen. Its recoil vibrated through her arms. The sharp odor of spent gunpowder seared her senses.

She'd shot a man. Maybe killed him. Yet she felt nothing.

She should move. See if he was still alive. Administer first aid. Something. Yet even though she was staring at his prone form, watching the dark stain seep through his sweatshirt and wick through the fabric like tie-dye, she couldn't quite believe what she'd done. None of it felt real.

Ripping her gaze from the crumpled form, she focused on her husband's pale face. "Alec?"

His gray eyes met hers. The shovel fell from his hands and clattered to the floor. In two strides he crossed the distance between them and gathered her in his arms. "Are you okay? Did they hurt you?"

She pressed her body against his warmth—warmth she'd thought she'd never feel again. "I'm fine." A bald-faced lie. She was trembling so hard she could hardly stand.

He moved back from her, running his gaze over her face and down to her bound hands. "The baby?" He smoothed a palm over her nightgown and the curve of her bulging abdomen.

"He's fine." She could feel him shifting inside her, his movements faster and more spastic than usual, as if fueled by the adrenaline in her bloodstream. "What is going on, Alec? Who are these men?"

He stepped away and grabbed a knife from the butcher block. Slipping the blade between her wrists, he cut the plastic binder, freeing her hands. One hand on the small of her back, he tried to guide her toward the garage. "We have to get out of here."

She stood rooted to the spot, still staring at the bodies on the floor. One slumped against the white kitchen cabinets clutching his bloody face, barely conscious enough to moan. The other lay sprawled where his body hit the floor. A pool of blood spread over the hardwood. "We have to call the police."

"No police."

"What do you mean, no police? Of course we have to call the police. These men broke in. They were going to kill me. I shot one of them, for crying out loud. He might be dead."

"I know you trust the police, but all cops aren't as honest as your dad was. We can't risk it."

"What do you mean?"

"I'll explain later. All of it. Right now we have to get out of here. The thug outside probably heard the gunshots."

"The thug outside? There's another?"

"He was waiting in a car down the street."

Mind still whirling, she let Alec guide her into the garage. She might not know what was going on, but she didn't want another of those men to catch up to them. She and Alec had been lucky to escape from the two in the kitchen. Before Alec had shown up, she'd thought she was dead.

Like Sally?

"One of those men said Sally is dead." Not wanting to believe it was true, she studied Alec's face, waiting for an expression that would answer her unspoken question.

He gave her a brief nod.

Pain clutched her heart. Her knees almost gave way beneath her. This couldn't be real. None of this could be happening.

Alec grasped her arm, keeping her on her feet and moving through the garage, toward the van. "Try not to think of it now. We have to focus on getting out of here."

She stopped in her tracks a step from the van. "Wait."

"Laura? Get in the van."

She glanced down at the Mak 9mm still in her fist. If they were going to face more of these men, she wanted to do it armed. "Rounds. We need bullets. And guns. The men in there have a mini arsenal on them."

"I'll get what I can. You get in the van."

"It'll take less time if I help."

He nodded toward the kitchen door and released her arm. "Let's make it quick."

They ducked back inside. The strong odor of blood filled Laura's senses and turned her stomach. She breathed shallowly through her mouth, trying to concentrate on getting the guns, trying to stave off the nausea, the way she had through the first and most of the second trimesters of her pregnancy.

The man Alec had laid out with the shovel hadn't moved. Except for the low groan rumbling deep in his throat, she might have thought he was dead. She was just about to kneel down and check him for weapons and rounds when Alec grabbed her arm. "I'll take care of him. You check the other one."

She nodded. She had to admit, she was relieved. There was something deathly brutal about this man. Every time he'd looked at her, she'd felt his hatred. His rage. Even though she'd never done anything to him. Even though she'd never even laid eyes on him before.

While Alec rifled through the man's clothes, she stepped across the floor to the man she'd shot. The pool of blood beneath him had grown, inching along the wood floor and seeping into the cracks between the boards. Blood soaked his sweatshirt around the exit hole in his back.

He was dead. She'd killed a man. Nausea bucked in her stomach. The coppery sweet odor clogged her throat, choking her. She struggled for breath. For control. She had to push the guilt away. She couldn't let herself feel. She had to function.

She bent down and picked up the pistol that had fallen from his hand. Then she focused on the man's waistband. Holding her breath, she ran her hand under his sweatshirt. She felt a pouch attached to his belt. She yanked up the sweatshirt's hem and unsnapped the pouch filled with 9mm rounds.

Alec handed her another pouch on his way to

the front of the house. Moments later he raced back into the kitchen empty handed. "We're going to have company. Get in the van. Hurry."

Scooping up the handgun and rounds, she scurried out the door and clambered into the van.

Alec took the driver's seat and started the engine. He snapped his seat belt and turned to her. "Keep your head down."

She hooked her own seat belt. Slipping out of the shoulder harness, she bent at the waist, her head nearly touching the dash, the baby pushing her stomach into her throat.

Alec hit the button of the garage door opener, shifted into Reverse and stomped on the gas.

The van lurched backward. They burst into the daylight. Laura lifted her head to peek through the window. A man strode through their front yard toward the driveway, an assault rifle in the ready position.

She ducked.

Gunfire popped, hitting steel, hitting glass. Cracks splintered the passenger window and spider-webbed the windshield. "Hold on," Alec shouted.

She hunkered lower. Grateful the lap belt was still in place, she gripped the bottom of the seat with one hand and braced against the dash with the other.

Reaching the bottom of the driveway, Alec slammed the car into drive. The van lurched. Rubber screeched against pavement, grabbing for purchase.

More gunfire from outside. The back window shattered.

The van thrust forward. Sitting as low as possible, Alec gripped the wheel, knuckles white, squinting through the cracked windshield. He spun around the bend at the mouth of the cul-de-sac. The van tilted, as if lifting off two wheels.

It settled on the straightaway. The engine roared, the sound overwhelming the thrum of Laura's pulse in her ears, the panic racing along her nerves.

Alec took two more turns before settling on the main road.

She sat upright in her seat and twisted to check out the blown-out back window. The road was vacant behind, no bullets flying, no car following. The wind whistled through the broken car windows and whipped her hair against her cheeks. Clutching dash and door, she closed her eyes.

This couldn't be happening. More than anything, she wanted to go to sleep, wake up and find she was safe in her bed. That Sally was still alive. That she had never pulled the trigger and taken a man's life. That it was all a vivid hormone-induced nightmare.

Opening her eyes, she focused on her husband. His shirt was ripped and bloodstained. And he hadn't injured his arm in the fight in the kitchen. She was sure of it. She touched his sleeve. "Are you okay?"

"I'm fine."

No, he wasn't fine. And despite what she'd said to reassure him earlier, neither was she. "What happened? How did you get hurt? Tell me what's going on."

Flattening his lips into a tight line, he took two more turns at top speed. He adjusted the wheel and settled on another country highway, pushing the pedal to the floor. "Now's not the best time."

She checked out the back window again. "No one's following. Now's the perfect time. Who were those men?"

A muscle flexed along his jaw.

"Do you know them?"

"Yes." His eyes narrowed and seemed to darken, turning gray to slate.

He knew, but he wasn't going to tell her. How could he not tell her? "They almost killed me. They were going to take our baby. I deserve to know who they are."

Eyes riveted to the road ahead, he blew out a long breath, as if acknowledging defeat. Another mile passed before he opened his mouth to speak. "You've heard of the Russian Mafiya."

Of course she had. She didn't have to have a father in law enforcement to be familiar with Russian organized crime. Their greed. Their brutality. Their blatant disregard for law and decency. And the men who had broken into their house and dragged her from her bed had spoken with Russian accents. But that still didn't explain anything. "Why would the Russian mob be after us?"

He hesitated again, this time his expression was one of pain. And guilt. "My name isn't Alec Martin."

"Excuse me?" Whatever she'd expected him to say, this wasn't close. Heat stole over her followed by cold. "What is your name?"

"Nikolai Stanislov."

"Russian." Her mind stuttered, struggling to process the information, struggling to make sense of it. "You're involved with the Russian mob?"

"Nika Stanislov was involved with the Russian mob."

Nika. His real name. She closed her eyes. She couldn't handle this. "That's why you use a false name? Because you're a mobster?"

"I'm not a mobster." He bit off the words, his voice sharp.

She opened her eyes and studied the lines of

his face, the bitter set to his jaw. He had the same short brown hair, the same gray eyes, the same rugged features, yet she didn't recognize this man. She'd been married to him for more than a year, dated him for two before that, and she didn't know him. "Who are you?"

"Alec Martin is a name assigned to me by the federal witness-security program."

"You're a crime witness?"

"Yes."

It didn't take much to put the pieces together. "You witnessed something having to do with Russian organized crime."

"My father is what they call a 'big man.'"

"Your father was a mafia don?"

"*Is.*"

"He's alive? You told me he died when you were young."

A bitter smile curved his lips. "Only in my fantasies."

She pressed her fingers against her lower lip. This couldn't be happening. The Alec she'd married was tender and honest. This Alec—the one who had another name, the one who knew mobsters, the one with fantasies of his father's death— she didn't *want* to know. "What crime did you witness?"

"You name it."

"Things your father did?"

"Yes."

"And you testified against him?"

He nodded slowly, his eyes still on the ribbon of asphalt stretching in front of them. "About thirteen years ago. He was convicted of manslaughter."

Manslaughter. Merely another name for murder.

"The men at the house were about my father getting revenge."

"If you testified against him thirteen years ago, why is he just coming after you now?"

"He was just released from prison."

"Why not put a contract out on you while he was in prison?"

"He likes to handle personal problems personally. Says it's a matter of honor. As if the son-of-a-bitch knows anything about honor. Those men weren't there to kill me. They were there to take me back to New York. Back to face my father."

"One of them was talking about taking our son." She slid her hands down over her belly. "What does your father want with our baby?"

"It doesn't matter what he wants. He's not going to get near our baby. I'll make sure of it."

She wanted to believe him, wanted it with her whole heart. But after what she'd been through today, she couldn't fool herself into thinking she and their son would be safe just because Alec said so. She couldn't fool herself into believing anything Alec—no, *Nika*—said. "Why didn't you tell me? When things became serious between us, when we started talking about marriage, about having kids…" Rage worked its way into her throat, pinching her voice, cutting off her words.

"I thought it was over. When I met you, nothing had happened for ten years. I thought I could finally have my own life, my own family."

"Did it ever occur to you that *I* should have a say in my future? Did it ever occur to you that *I* might have ideas about the type of man I wanted to marry? The type of man I wanted to father my kids?" A flurry of kicks vibrated inside her, her son's movement fueled by the adrenaline racing through her veins. She folded her hands over her belly and lowered her voice. "Did you ever consider giving me a choice?"

"We chose each other, Laura. Our feelings for each other had nothing to do with my background. That hasn't changed."

"Everything's changed."

"Because my past is different than you thought?"

"Because my future is different. Our son's future is different."

This morning when she'd awakened, her life had been everything she'd ever wanted. She had a thriving business. She thought she was married to the man of her dreams. And she had a perfect little son on the way. Her biggest problem had been a case of the sniffles. Her biggest concern had been asking Sally to open the bar so she could get a little extra sleep. And now her friend, her marriage—everything she knew—was gone.

Her sinuses burned. Tears stung her eyes. She wanted to scream. To hit him. To hurt him. To make him see what he'd done to her, to their baby. "This is not what I wanted. Not for myself, and certainly not for my son."

"I know."

"Do you? I wonder. Did you know that my mother used to stay up all night whenever my father was on patrol? She would sit in the dark with her rosary beads and wait for him. I think she truly believed if she didn't keep her prayer vigil, he wouldn't come home to us."

Alec said nothing.

But what could he say? He knew about her mother's fears. He'd seen for himself how her anxiety had gotten so severe before her death that she'd had to live in an institution. But even then, Laura had doubted he'd truly understood the causes and ripple effects of her mother's illness.

Now she was certain he hadn't understood. Not one bit. If he had, he never could have kept his real identity from her. He never could have put her in this position. "I always tried to stay awake with her. When I fell asleep, I felt so guilty. Like I'd let her down."

"That's terrible to put so much pressure on a kid."

"Our son is going to face more pressure than that. If he survives long enough to be born, that is."

She wiped her cheeks with the back of one hand then buried her clenched fist in her lap. "By the time I reached high school, I decided that my life was going to be different. I would *make* it different. I set out to choose a man with a safe job to fall in love with. To marry. To have a child with. I didn't even date men who didn't fit into that plan. I didn't look at them twice. When I met you, I thought I'd found the perfect man. A liquor distributor. A salesman. Not a police officer, like my father. And sure as hell not the son of a mobster. If I'd had any idea…"

The creases flanking his mouth and digging into his forehead deepened. "I wanted to be your husband. I wanted it so much."

"Enough to lie to me?"

"I didn't lie."

"You didn't tell me who you really were. That's lying in my book."

"You're right. I'm sorry."

But his acquiescence wasn't enough to loosen the knot twisting in her stomach or lighten the weight in her chest. It wasn't even close. "You should have told me the truth, Alec or Nikolai or whatever-the-hell your name is. You should have let *me* decide if I wanted to live with this ticking bomb."

"I'm sorry, Laura. I was afraid you wouldn't want me. Not if you knew who I was." He pulled his gaze from the highway for a moment and looked at her. "I didn't want to lose you."

"Damn you, Alec. You've lost me, anyway."

Alec turned hollow eyes on the road twisting through rolling farm fields, his face pale in the shattered pattern of sunlight shining through the windshield.

She clutched the bottom of her nightgown, trying to cover her legs. If only she could do something. Take control. Stand up, walk around, burn off the desperate feeling storming her nerves. Anything. Instead she was stuck in this damn car next to a man she didn't know, driving hell-bent for nowhere. And there wasn't a thing she could do to change it. Or was there? "Turn the car around."

"What?"

"I want to go back to Beaver Falls. I want you to drop me off at the police station."

Chapter Four

Alec gripped the steering wheel. His head throbbed just behind his eyes. Dread pooled in his chest, filling his lungs, making it hard to breathe. "I'm not taking you back to Beaver Falls."

"Why not?"

"I don't trust the police."

"Why?"

"My father has been successful because he knows that most people have a price, and he can afford to pay it."

"You think he's bribing police officers in Beaver Falls?" She sounded shocked, like this was the most outrageous suggestion she'd ever heard.

He shouldn't be surprised. "You only think it's ridiculous because your father was a cop. You come from a totally different world than I do. You automatically trust cops. You see them as the good guys, the white knights."

"And your background makes you objective?" She shook her head. "Just because your father bribed cops in New York when you were growing up, doesn't mean all the officers in the entire country are on his payroll."

"Maybe not. But the trick is finding out which ones are. *Before* you trust them."

"Do you have any reason to believe the Beaver Falls police are corrupt? Do you have any proof?"

"I have a feeling."

"A feeling?"

"Yes. And in light of what's happened, a feeling is enough. We can't take chances."

"I'm not taking chances. I'm just not going to let your paranoia prevent me from getting help." *Or from leaving you.* She hadn't said it, but the sentiment was there, hanging in the air between them like an iron curtain.

"It's not paranoia."

"Really? You haven't given me one reason I shouldn't rely on the Beaver Falls police."

"Before I found Sally and the others, I called 911. I reported the gas leak and—"

"The others?"

Alec cringed. He had forgotten Laura didn't know about the massacre he'd stumbled across. The deaths. The explosion. "I went to the restaurant to look for you. That's where I found Sally."

"And others." The words came out on a whisper, as if she was afraid to know more, but couldn't keep herself from asking.

"Yes. There were others."

"Who?"

He'd give anything not to tell her. The news of Sally's death was enough for Laura to come to terms with. But knowing Laura, she would never let it go. Not until she knew everything. "Your prep cook, Tim."

She flinched as if he'd physically hit her.

"One of your waitresses."

"Traci. Traci was supposed to open the dining room for lunch." Her voice was robotic, as if she was keeping the names at a distance, not really thinking about what it all meant. "No one else. Please, no one else."

"The guy that works for the produce company."

"Ed."

"I didn't see anyone else." As if the three he'd just named plus Sally weren't enough.

She leaned back in her seat, breathing shallowly through her mouth. The only sound inside the van was the thrashing wind and the miles humming by under the tires.

Finally she turned her head toward him. "What does any of this have to do with not trusting the police?"

"I smelled a gas leak when I entered the building. I called 911. About the leak. About my suspicion that there was more going on. The police never showed. Not the entire time I was there."

"Because their response time wasn't as fast as you thought it should be, you assume the entire Beaver Falls Police Department is working for your father?"

She made him sound like he *was* paranoid. "It wouldn't have to be the entire department. It could be one or two officers that delayed their response. Or the dispatcher. But I guarantee it wasn't a coincidence that the police didn't arrive before the gas explosion and fire destroyed evidence of the murders."

"The restaurant exploded?" She gasped in a breath, weathering the shock as she had the news of the deaths.

Alec watched her out of the corner of his eye. There was no telling how these shocks, one after another, would affect her health. At just over seven months along, it couldn't be good for her. Or for the baby. He'd heard enough stories of premature labor to scare the piss out of him.

But short of lying, he didn't know how to protect her from the truth. And he'd lied to Laura enough. More lies, even to protect her, would only make things worse. "I know this whole thing seems insane. It's only natural you'd want to go to the police, to trust them. Especially since your father was a cop. But if you knew *my* father, if you'd seen what he's capable of…"

"I've seen enough to know we can't handle this alone."

She might be right. God knew he'd come awfully close to losing everything this morning, closer than he could bear thinking about. But who the hell *could* they trust? In his father's world, trust was for dead men. And whether he liked it or not, this morning he'd been sucked back into his father's world. And so had Laura. "We don't have a choice. We have to handle this alone."

She shook her head, as if she couldn't imagine it.

She probably couldn't. She was raised by a cop, taught to trust cops. He wasn't. And the one time he'd trusted the authorities, they'd let him down. It had taken ten years, but they let him down nonetheless. "I understand you're angry with me. Hell, you probably hate me. That's okay. I deserve it. But you need to think beyond that. You have to trust me. You have no other choice."

"No. I have a choice." She narrowed her eyes to brown slits and set her chin. "I don't trust you.

I don't even know you. I want out. Now. Take me to the police station."

He tightened his grip on the steering wheel until his knuckles ached. "Like hell."

"You're kidnapping me?"

"Damn it, Laura. I'm not staking our lives on the police. If that means I'm kidnapping you, so be it."

She reached toward him. Before he realized what she was doing, she unsnapped his cell phone from his belt. She flipped the phone open. "Now do you want to drop me off at the station, or should we do this the hard way?"

Alec gritted his teeth. He could just pull the car over and wrestle the phone from her before she had a chance to punch in 911, but somehow he couldn't bring himself to do it. Not to Laura. "All right. Call them."

She raised her eyebrows.

"Tell them to meet you in an hour at Conason Park. Near the shelter."

"What are you up to?"

He didn't answer. She'd understand soon enough. If his plan worked, either Laura would be as safe as possible with the cops or as safe as possible with him. And all that mattered now was that she and the baby were as safe as they could be. "Make the call."

LAURA JOINED ALEC on the edge of the bluff overlooking Bear River and the Conason Park shelter. A cool wind gushed through the valley and swirled over the bluffs. Laura shivered and pulled the blanket, rummaged from the winter driving supplies in the van, tighter around her nightgown. She hadn't felt cold since she'd become pregnant. Through the Wisconsin winter she'd worn short-sleeved tops most days. But even though she wasn't exactly dressed, the chill she felt now went deeper than any clothing or blanket could warm. It drilled into the very marrow of her bones.

She wanted to get this over with. Leaving the life she'd thought she had, the husband she thought she knew, was painful enough. The last thing she wanted to do was draw it out. But Alec had insisted they stay on top of the bluff, watch for the police's arrival and make sure his father's thugs were nowhere in sight before he would let her go.

Shading her eyes with one hand, she peered down into the valley. Noon sun sparkled off the river that wound through the park. Maples and oaks had yet to leaf out, and their bare branches camouflaged little of the parking lot, playground and shelter below. From here they could see the park entrances and roads approaching the shelter in both directions. If something wasn't on the up-and-up, they would see it.

It seemed Alec had thought of everything.

No surprise. She'd always known he was smart. His intelligence was one of the things that attracted her to him the first time he'd shown up at her newly established restaurant to take her liquor order. What she hadn't recognized was his cunning. She'd never guessed he could think like a criminal, anticipate what they would do, how they would strike.

But then, she hadn't known so many things about him.

He stood next to her, eyes shifting back and forth, covering both entrances of the park. Tension rolled off him in waves. His body seemed to vibrate with restlessness.

He'd always carried a certain intensity, a need to move, ever since she'd met him. If seated, he'd jiggle his leg. If standing, he'd pace. More than once, she'd jokingly asked him why he needed to keep moving, what he was running from.

Now she knew.

"Where will you go?" The question escaped her lips before she could bite it back. She probably shouldn't have asked it. She probably shouldn't care.

He didn't look at her, his concentration rooted

to the park. "I don't know. Maybe the Twin Cities. Maybe farther. Somewhere I can get lost in the crowds."

"Your money won't last long in a city."

"I'll find work. Off the books."

That was easy enough. Although she never used undocumented workers, she knew countless other businesses did. There were a lot of advantages for the business owner. Low wages. No need to provide health care and other benefits. And no unemployment, worker's compensation or payroll tax. The underground economy was alive and well in the U.S. It was certainly possible for Alec to simply vanish from the system. She would never see him again.

And he would never know their son.

She steeled herself against the thought. Alec had made his bed when he'd decided to lie to her about who he really was. She couldn't let herself feel sorry for him. She wouldn't. But still, the idea that he would miss his son's birth, his first words, his first steps, left a hollow feeling in her chest.

But even worse, their son wouldn't have a dad.

As much stress as her father's job had caused during her childhood, she couldn't have imagined growing up without him. His encouragement. His unwavering faith in her. His love.

She wanted those things for her child. When

she'd chosen to marry Alec, she'd done so as much for their future children as she had for herself. She'd thought he'd be a gentle and caring father. A protector who would keep them safe. A role model.

How could she have been so wrong?

She couldn't think about it. None of this was in her control. Alec's lies had rendered all her plans useless. All her dreams of a happy family unattainable. She just had to do the best she could from here on out. "What am I supposed to tell the baby about you?"

"Nothing."

"I have to tell him something. He deserves to know."

"I don't want him to be part of that world. My father's world. I don't want him to know anything about it." Muscles clenched at the corners of his jaw. Tendons stood out along his neck. "If everything works out with the police the way you're hoping it will, promise me you'll tell him I'm dead."

"I'm not going to lie."

"You don't know it will be a lie."

His words knocked the air from her lungs. He was right. She wouldn't know. His father could find him, kill him, and she would never know.

"Promise me."

Tightness pinched her throat. Swallowing hard, she smoothed her hair back from her face and scanned the park through the haze of leafless branches. "I'll tell him you're dead."

"Good."

Where were the police? Why weren't they here by now?

As if conjured by her thoughts, a sedan slowed on the highway below. It swung into the entrance of the park and crept toward the parking lot. She'd never cared about makes and models of cars, couldn't tell one from another, but the plain lines and dark blue of this one seemed like just the type the police favored for their unmarked cars.

The time had come.

She forced herself to keep her eyes on the car. She couldn't allow herself to glance at Alec, to look one last time at the intense gray of his eyes, the gentle hook of his nose, the full lips she'd once relished kissing. It wouldn't get her anywhere. It would only make the moment more bitter. Only remind her of what she'd once thought she'd had with him. What she'd never really had at all.

The car wound past the first parking lot and toward the shelter.

"There's a cabin up near Minoqua. On Lake Tomahawk. 1342 Brinberry Road." She could feel his gaze on her, sense the question in his eyes. "It was my dad's fishing and hunting cabin. The one in pictures of me as a kid. Before he died, he sold it to his former partner. No one uses it until summer, so it should be empty this time of year. The key is hanging under the edge of the siding, near the door."

He nodded. "Thanks."

The car slowed near a bank of trees.

Drawing a deep breath of resolve, Laura offered her gun to Alec, grip first.

Alec met it with a flat palm, pushing the weapon back to her. "Keep it."

"I won't be able to keep it. Not in police custody." She looked up at him. But he was watching the car. She followed his gaze.

The car had come to a complete stop. Now it backed into a small, gravel service path concealed by trees on one side, and the park shelter on the other. A beam of sunlight penetrated the windshield, shining like a spotlight on the occupants.

Laura narrowed her eyes, straining to see. The driver looked young, not familiar. But the passenger—

She let out the breath she hadn't realized she'd been holding and stared at the cut and bloodied face of the man who had dragged her from her bed. The man who had said he'd killed Sally.

Sergei Komorov.

"Do you still think the Beaver Falls Police Department will protect you?" Alec said, his voice as low and ominous as a rumble of thunder.

Her mind spun. She didn't know what to think anymore. All she knew was that there would be no officers whisking her and her baby to safety. There *was* no safety anymore.

For any of them.

Chapter Five

Evening shadows slid into the forest as Laura ran her hand under the edge of the cabin's siding. Except for their time at the park, she'd spent all day in the van. And even though her belly was awkwardly in the way, it felt good to bend and stretch out her hamstrings. Her fingers brushed rough wood and swiped through webs and sticky egg sacks left by last year's crop of spiders. She shivered, but kept groping until her fingers hit a protruding nail. She slid her fingers down the nail, gripped the key and slipped it free. At least the key's hiding spot hadn't changed. Pushing herself to her feet, she circled to the door.

Other than the crackle of sticks under Alec's feet as he walked around the cabin's perimeter, the forest was silent. In summer, the song of frogs along the lakeshore and the chirp of crickets filled the dusk, finally giving way to the haunting calls of loons late into the night. But in April the lake was just waking up from winter, and only the birds broke their silence.

She slipped the key into the lock. Rusty tumblers ground and scraped as the dead bolt slid open. Alec had said he wanted to collect firewood to ward off the north woods chill before he joined her in the cabin. But Laura knew his real motivation for exploring the forest surrounding the cabin had more to do with security than warmth. It was just as well. She hadn't set foot in the cabin since her father had become sick. And with the uncertain way she felt about Alec, she'd rather confront the house and her memories alone.

She turned the knob and pushed. Hinges creaked as it swung wide. Picking up the bags of groceries, clothing and bandages for Alec's arm Alec had bought at a Wal-Mart on the way out of Beaver Falls, she stepped onto the worn white-and-yellow-patterned linoleum she remembered from childhood.

Her mother's deep-gold curtains had been replaced with a cheery yellow-and-red check, but the rest of the kitchen appeared untouched. Leave it to Frank to keep the same decor. He probably couldn't bring himself to change anything his former partner had picked out unless he was forced.

Laura breathed in the faint scent of mildew

and mothballs. Even that hadn't changed. She remembered stashing mothballs around the cabin before winter to keep the mice out. Apparently, that strategy still worked.

Setting the bags on the kitchen counter, she pulled out the maternity clothing, undergarments and shoes Alec had bought, and stepped through the archway leading into the cabin's only other room. This room, too, was just as she remembered. Sure there were a few new sticks of furniture: a pleather recliner, a sofa bed near the wood-burning stove. But the ancient couch still dominated the room that doubled as gathering area and bedroom, its orange stripes as vibrantly loud as ever. The Bengal tiger of couches, her dad used to call it.

The smell in here hadn't changed, either. Wood fire mixed with a curious blend of stale cigar smoke and the ever-present moth balls. She inhaled deeply, letting her gaze wander over the log walls, the deer antlers mounted on plaques. The stuffed muskie immortalized in midleap. The built-in gun cabinet her father had once filled with hunting rifles and hand guns long since sold. Guns her father had taught her to use.

She crossed to the cabinet. Although Frank had taken his hunting rifles home for the winter, the deluxe cleaning and maintenance kit remained in the drawer beneath the cabinet's glass doors. After donning a pink smocklike top and stretchy maternity jeans, she gathered her gun and the cleaning kit from the drawer and carried all of it to the screened-in porch.

Two old couches still lined the porch and kept watch over the lake at the bottom of the wooded slope. She lowered herself onto one and spread the cleaning kit on the coffee table made from an old telephone cable spool. She unloaded the Mak's clip and started breaking the pistol down.

Her fingers trembled, making the task difficult, but as she took the pieces apart and assembled the cleaning rod, she listened to the slow lap of the lake against the pier footings. The scent of burned gunpowder mixed with the almost imperceptible breeze. She inhaled deeply, the scents bringing back feelings from another time. A safer time.

She'd learned to clean a gun on this porch. Her dad had shown her how to break down a weapon, to stack two patches together to create a tight swab, to clean the barrel from breech to muzzle. He'd taught her to shoot here at the lake, as well, first with hunting rifles, then with handguns. She remembered his patient lessons, the way he'd shown her how to hold a gun, to squeeze the trigger instead of yanking it. She'd practiced for hours, until she could put a round right between the yellow cartoon eyes on a cat food can.

She pinched two patches and threaded them into the tip, creating a swab. By the time she ran the cleaning rod down the barrel and attached the tip, her hands were no longer shaking. Grasping the bottle of solvent, she twisted off the cover. The familiar oily yet turpentine-sweet scent seemed to clear her head and slow her heartbeat. As she twisted the swab into the chamber, the mundane act quieted the helpless jangle of her nerves.

She pulled the swab through the barrel in the direction of the bullet and then reached for the bore brush. She was in control. She could take apart the weapon, clean it, put it back together. Just like her father had taught her. Here in this cabin, surrounded by the scents of lake and solvent and those damned moth balls, performing the ordinary routine of maintaining her weapon, here she could handle things. Here she was in control. And after today, she needed that feeling more than she needed air.

The screen door snapped in the kitchen, wood cracking against wood.

She jumped at the sound. She knew it had to be Alec entering the cabin. But that thought didn't calm her jangling nerves. Her hands began to tremble again.

The cabin's floorboards creaked under the

weight of footfalls, followed by the thunk of logs dropping into the box next to the wood stove. Minute after minute passed while he rustled in the kitchen and moved around the cabin. Finally the sounds ceased.

She didn't have to peer over her shoulder to know he stood in the doorway. She could feel his gaze. She could hear the gentle pulse of his breathing. Her chest tightened.

"How are you holding up?" Alec's baritone rippled over her skin.

"As well as can be expected." Her fingers moved faster, turning the cleaning rod, pulling the swab through the barrel.

"I checked the area. A cabin at the end of the road looks occupied, but other than that, we seem to have this part of the lake to ourselves."

She nodded, keeping her focus on her work.

"I'll keep watch tonight, just in case. You'd better get some sleep."

"Sleep. Right."

He stepped onto the porch, the floorboards squeaking slightly. The couch beside her dipped under his weight. Even without looking at him, she could see he'd changed into the new clothes they'd bought. A deep-blue Henley replaced the tattered and bloody dress shirt. A pair of jeans molded to his thighs like a second skin.

"Do you need me to bandage your arm?"

"I managed."

She almost sighed with relief. She didn't want to touch him, to care for his wound. After all she'd learned today, she wasn't feeling very caring.

He pulled his Mak from his waistband, removed the magazine and checked the gun to make sure it was unloaded. Then he began breaking it down. His fingers moved quick and sure, the movements second nature.

Laura's own hands stilled. "You told me you didn't like guns."

Alec kept working, plucking another cleaning rod from the kit and fitting it together. "I don't."

"You seem to know your way around that Mak."

"I know guns. That doesn't mean I like them. I learned about them when I was young. Like you did."

Her gut clenched. "My father taught me to shoot so I could protect myself."

"So did mine."

The thought that he was comparing his childhood experiences to hers made her sick to her stomach. "Did he really? Or did he teach you with the hope that you'd be a hit man someday?" She knew her words were sharp, cruel. But she didn't try to take them back.

He didn't flinch. "Probably both." His voice was matter-of-fact, as if he was describing how his father always hoped he'd play football or perform in the school band. Yet bitterness and anger hardened his muscles and throbbed in the air around him.

"What happened, when you were a kid?"

"You mean how did I learn about guns?"

"How did you come to send your father to prison?"

He jammed a swab into the cleaning rod's tip. "I saw my father kill someone. I testified against him and one of his thugs." His words hung in the air like an unfinished song.

"That's it?"

"That's it."

There was more he wasn't telling her. She could feel it. "And you went to the police?"

"I went to the FBI. My father owned a lot of the police force. I never knew who was on the take and who was clean."

She nodded. Of course. The source of Alec's belief that all police worked for his father. Of course, in Beaver Falls it had been true.

"I gave them everything I knew. Everything I'd seen about my father's businesses growing up."

"And you testified against him?"

"As it turned out, the federal charges were

dismissed. Even with my testimony, they couldn't find enough evidence to make them stick."

"But he went to prison."

"He and the thug were convicted by the state for manslaughter."

"And they're both out."

"Yes."

She thought of the man in the kitchen, the one Alec had hit with the shovel. The one who claimed he'd slit Sally's throat. "The other man. Was he at our house?"

"Yes."

"The one you didn't want me to search for weapons."

"Sergei Komorov."

Nausea surged into her throat at the name. At what he'd said he'd done. She focused on the gun barrel. She couldn't think about Sally right now, couldn't think about their employees or the destruction of the Blue Ox. If she did, she wouldn't be able to go on. "So after you testified you joined the witness-security program."

She could feel his nod more than see it. "They gave me the chance for a new life, and I took it."

"And that's how you ended up in Wisconsin selling liquor to restaurants."

"And that led to meeting you."

"And marrying me, never telling me who you really were." She plucked the dirty patches from the cleaning rod, trying to control the stir of emotion inside her.

"I fell in love with you the first time I saw you, Laura. It was the way you looked at me. As if I was a better man than I ever thought possible. By the time you agreed to marry me, I'd convinced myself I was that man."

Tears of frustration burned in her eyes. She fought them back. "What about the man you *are*, Alec? Who is *that* man?"

"I'm not my father's son, if that's what you think."

"I don't know what to think. I used to believe in you. In us. But everything I believed turned out to be wrong."

"Not everything. I love you, Laura. Nothing could ever change that."

His words settled in her chest like a dull ache. She focused on the patches in her fingers, exposing clean surfaces, pinching them, threading them into the rod's tip as best she could. "You don't lie to someone you love."

He didn't answer.

She didn't know what to say, either. She didn't know this man. The Alec Martin she thought she married would never lie. He would never betray her like this. God help her, she didn't even know if Alec Martin existed, or if he was a product of Nika Stanislov's lies and her willing imagination.

Whoever this man was, one thing was clear. Despite all her plans for her life, she'd ended up in a situation that was far worse than even her mother had dared to fear. A situation she might never escape. "What are we going to *do?*" Her words were barely a whisper, but they screamed with the force of her fear.

Alec looked at the gun in his hands. "God, Laura. I don't know."

"It never occurred to you he might find you when he got out of prison? You don't have any kind of plan?"

"I should have stashed cash somewhere. I should have gotten extra identification. I should have planned for this." He set the gun on the table and raked his hands through his hair, elbows braced on knees. "Why didn't I plan for this?"

He rubbed his forehead as if trying to summon the answer. "The Witness Security Program has never lost a witness. Not when the witness has cut off all ties with the past. Not when they've followed the rules. I assumed that's the way it would be for me, too. I trusted…"

"You have no plan for getting us out of this."

He dropped his arms to his lap. Sitting up

straight, he swiveled to face her. "We run. Disappear."

"Until he finds us the next time."

"We'll make sure he doesn't."

"How is that a way to live? To raise a child?"

A muscle ticked along his jaw. "I don't see there's any other choice. Do you have any ideas?"

She could only think of one. "We go to the police."

"After what happened in Beaver Falls?"

"Your father can't pay off every police officer in Wisconsin."

"No. But he can find out which cops are protecting us and pay *them* off."

"We'll find someone trustworthy."

"Do you have anyone in mind?"

She didn't. All the officers she knew that had served with her father were retired. Or dead. "We find someone."

"And how are we going to do that?"

Her fingers trembled. She tried to fit the too-loose patch into the barrel, but failed. It flopped on the end of the cleaning rod, waving like a white flag of surrender.

Taking the rod and barrel from her hand, Alec set them on the table. He covered her fists, cupping them in his palms. His hands felt so warm, so steady, so right. The way they had when he'd slipped the ring on her finger. When he'd pledged his life to her. When she'd pledged hers to him.

She ached to lean toward him. If she did, she knew he'd take her in his arms. She knew how his embrace would feel, strong and safe. Like the feeling he gave her when they made love, when she'd grip his biceps and hold on as he drove into her, as he claimed her for his own.

A shiver shuddered over her skin. She'd give anything to belong to him like that now. But she couldn't. She'd lost too much. Far too much. Her belief in him. Her trust. He'd taken them from her.

And a simple touch wouldn't bring them back.

She pulled her hands from his grasp and wrapped her arms around her abdomen. Turning away, she looked out the screens at the bows of pine framing the twilight-touched water. "I need some time alone."

Only the sound of the lapping waves broke the silence between them. Finally he picked up the pieces of his gun and stood. "I just wanted to make sure you were okay." A long minute passed before he turned away. He stepped into the cabin and closed the door behind him, leaving her on the porch.

Laura pulled an old blanket around her shoulders and tried to turn her attention to cleaning her weapon, to the scent of the solvent, to the feeling of control she'd claimed as a kid. But it was no use. That world was part of the past. The memories of her dad, of all he'd taught her, of all the cabin had once meant to her, had given her a strong foundation. But none of it could change the way things were now.

Tears blurred her vision. And out in the darkness, the lonely sound of a loon's laugh echoed across the water.

Chapter Six

Alec stood with his back to the door and rubbed his eyes with thumb and forefinger until multicolored stars exploded behind his lids. He'd tried to explain himself to Laura. Tried to make her see why he'd done the things he had. Tried to help her face things he'd never until now forced himself to face.

It hadn't worked.

He rubbed his eyes harder. If only he could erase the image of her wrapping her arms around her belly as if shielding their child from him. As if *he* was the danger. As if *he* was the enemy she had to fight. But he couldn't erase it. Even through the explosion of color behind closed lids, he could see her fear, her anger, her mistrust.

Emotions he'd put there. Emotions he couldn't change. All he could do now was keep Laura and their baby safe. And he would use anything at his disposal to make sure that's exactly what he did.

Striding the length of the cabin, he stepped into the kitchen, grasped his cell phone from his belt and checked the battery readout. Low. Very low. If he was lucky, it would be good for a call or two and that was it. He wished he'd thought of buying a charger when they'd stopped for clothing, supplies and cash on the way out of Beaver Falls. Now they couldn't risk using a credit card. Now that they'd left Beaver Falls, they couldn't afford to do anything that would leave a trail. They had to stay invisible from here on out. He would have to use some of their limited supply of cash.

He punched in Wayne's cell number and held the phone to his ear.

His old friend answered on the second ring. "Bigelow."

"Where are you?"

"Nika. So glad to hear from you." His breath roared in the phone, punching between his words. "I'm in Madison. I decided to send myself to cover Tony Griggs's death."

"Learn anything from your contacts in the FBI?"

"You know the feds. Their lips are as tight as their sphincters. Besides, they're not on the case. It's being handled locally."

"Locally? The murder of a U.S. marshal?"

"The guy was retired."

"What does that matter? He was killed to get to me. He was killed because of his job."

"But they don't know that."

"Then tell them, goddamn it!"

"You know that means nothing coming from me. You're going to have to tell them yourself."

Bigelow was right, and Alec knew it. His father would be careful not to leave evidence suggesting the motive behind Griggs's murder. And without evidence, the crime would appear to be a garden-variety murder. Although brutal, it would be a case squarely under the jurisdiction of the state. "So in the meantime, my father pays some flatfoot to look the other way."

"I don't think the detective in charge of the case is on the take."

"What makes you think that?"

"I don't know. A feeling. He seems like a straight shooter."

"Seems like a straight shooter?" Alec almost pulled the phone away from his ear and stared into it. He expected Laura to trust the police. He didn't expect the same from a cynical curmudgeon like Bigelow. Hell, Bigelow had more experience sniffing out cops on the take than he did. "When did you put on the rose-colored glasses?"

"Listen, his name is Mylinski. He lives in a crappy house and drives a crappy car. His idea of a night out is drinking a beer at the local brew pub. This guy isn't on Ivan Stanislov's payroll."

"So you think he's going to actually investigate?"

"Sure. But I'm sure he could use some help. You could provide that help."

Alec stared at the door leading to the screened porch. As much as his father deserved to be thrown straight back into prison, he couldn't risk Laura and the baby to make sure it happened. He and Laura had to disappear. Driving to Wisconsin's capitol city and meeting with police wasn't exactly disappearing. "No. I've trusted the police all I'm going to."

"The FBI, then. I've been talking to this guy, Callahan. He's part of the FBI's ROC unit."

Alec shook his head and paced across the tiny kitchen floor. "If I get involved with this investigation, how long do you think it would take my father to find us? It would be like waving a red flag at a bull."

"Us?"

Alec stopped dead. Damn slip of the tongue. He had to be more careful about the words he chose. Not that this slip mattered. Bigelow had never let him down before. And besides, Alec's father already knew about Laura. "I have a wife. Sergei Komorov almost killed her today."

"Komorov? Damn. I'm sorry to hear your wife had to run into him. She okay?"

"Yeah, she's okay." At least physically. Their marriage, on the other hand, was a different story. "I'm not dragging her into my father's line of fire."

"Understandable. But will she really be safe with your father free?"

An uneasy feeling niggled at the back of his neck. "You seem a little eager. What's in this for you?"

"An exclusive, of course. Maybe I'll write a book. I help you, you help me. Just like old times."

Old times. Whoever said they were the best times had never lived in Alec's shoes. But there was no use in denying his past. Not anymore. And although seeing the love die in Laura's eyes had diced his heart like a damned Cuisinart, there was a certain sense of relief now that she knew where he'd come from.

All that was left was to keep her safe. But no matter how tempting it was to lend a hand to sending his father back to a cell, his priority had to be Laura and their son. "You'll have to find something else to write your book about, Bigelow. We'll be laying low."

"You sure?"

"I'm sure."

He was about to punch the off switch when he heard Bigelow's voice. "Nika?"

"Yeah?"

"Congratulations."

"For what?"

"Your marriage. If I'd known, I would've sent a card."

SERGEI KOMOROV took a slug of Stolichnaya and cursed the pounding in his skull. If he was lucky, the vodka would wash it away along with dousing the fire cutting across his nose and cheek. If he was really lucky and he drank enough, it might even drown his shame.

He still couldn't believe that Nika had laid him out with a damned shovel. Nika, who wasn't worth his spit. Nika who was nothing but a *musor.* A rat. A piece of garbage.

He shook his head, causing another eruption of pain that flattened him against the car's seat. Nika never deserved to be Ivan's son. The place Ivan reserved for him should have belonged to Sergei. Instead, for all his effort and loyalty, Sergei had gotten ten years in prison. Ten years of being cut out of the action. Ten years of the sun's rays falling on someone else.

Ivan was bitter toward his son's betrayal. But

at least Ivan could run the empire he'd built from prison. At least he had an empire to return to. Nika's betrayal had left Sergei with nothing. Nothing but Ivan's charity.

His cell phone's shrill tune cut through the purr of the sedan's engine. News of Nika, he hoped. He fished the phone out of the pocket of his leather coat and flipped it open. "Yeah."

"My son went north." Ivan's thick accent sounded as close as if he was sitting next to Sergei in the sedan.

"Where?"

"Cellular phone signals are not so precise. If they were, I wouldn't need you."

The verbal slap stung more than the cut on Sergei's face. He scoured his aching head for answers. He'd looked through everything at Nika's home worth looking through. Trinkets. Photo albums. Old letters. If his head would stop throbbing, he could think. He needed something to lead to their location. Someplace secluded. Someplace Nika would feel safe.

Or someplace his wife would feel safe. "I have an idea."

"Good. Is Pavel with you?"

Sergei glanced at the little worm driving the car, his wire-rimmed glasses reflecting the sun. If Pavel Tverdovsky had been in the house instead of hunkered down in the car playing with his computer, Nika would be bound and gagged in the trunk right now. "He's here."

"Good."

A twinge of anger made Sergei's lips twist in a snarl. Pavel the wunderkind had allowed Nika to escape. But it wouldn't be only Pavel who paid the price if they didn't bring Nika back to Ivan.

"And Oleg?"

"Dead." The woman probably thought she'd killed him. Probably was feeling guilty about it. Wouldn't she be surprised to learn Sergei himself had put the final bullet in Oleg's brain rather than risk taking him to a hospital? That he and Pavel had dumped the body deep in the forest where he wouldn't be found?

"No more screw-ups, Sergei. If you bring my son and my grandson home, the rest is yours."

The woman. Sergei smiled despite the pain. Tipping the bottle to his lips, he drank deep, thoughts of bruising the blonde's pretty face as Nika watched almost as appealing as the vodka coursing down his throat.

The doctor they'd found to sew him back together had told him to take it easy, to let his concussion heal, to give his lacerated face some time. What the hell did he know? Sergei had waited long enough. Now he was going to make Nika wish he'd never run to the FBI. He was going to bring the *musor* to his knees.

ALEC EASED THE SCREEN DOOR closed behind him and stepped out into the cool night air to take another look around. Laura had finally fallen asleep on the sofa bed, her breathing growing deep and regular. Good thing. After all she'd been through, she had to be exhausted. He, on the other hand, was glad he had a reason to avoid sleep. Even awake he kept seeing visions of Sally's battered face and bloody hair. But as the night wore on, her eyes grew less blue in his visions and more brown—like Laura's.

He needed to walk, to pace, to work off some of the energy storming his nerves. And his hourly check of the cabin's perimeter was the perfect opportunity.

He walked slowly, pistol in hand, scanning the silhouettes of trees and bushes. Moonlight filtered through evergreen branches and glinted off the van's windshield, making the cracks sparkle like facets of a diamond.

He circled the cabin and walked down the steep slope leading to the water. The light breeze had died, leaving the air cold and still. The lake at the bottom of the wooded slope reflected the moon and stars as clearly as a mirror.

He completed his trek around the cabin and strode to the end of the gravel drive that led to the road. Running parallel to the highway, the narrow road wound through trees, cresting and dipping with the topography. From his earlier scouting trip, he knew that one end of the road dead ended at the tip of a small peninsula that jutted into the lake. About a dozen cabins lined the road, most dark and still and vacant. Only the end cabin appeared to be occupied, besides theirs.

He walked a short distance up the road, breathing in the cold night air. He had just started back to the cabin when the whoosh of speeding tires on the highway cut through the silence like a machete. He spun around and peered through the trees.

Headlights swept over him as a car swung onto the twisting gravel road.

A shot of adrenaline jump-started his pulse. Three in the morning was a little late for lake residents to be returning home. Especially since the taverns had to close by two. They might be teenagers looking for a place to park. That would be logical. But somehow, as much as he wished there was some sort of innocent explanation, he couldn't believe it. He started jogging for the cabin, keeping one eye on the headlights.

The car took the first bend in the winding road that circled this little bay off the larger lake. Then suddenly the headlights vanished, and only the engine's purr still wound through the trees.

Heart knocking hard, Alec raced for the cabin. That car wasn't filled with necking teenagers and it sure as hell wasn't returning from a night on the town. He didn't have a second to waste. He and Laura had to get out of here, and they had to do it now.

Chapter Seven

The squeak of the screen door wound its way into Laura's dreams. She jolted into a sitting position, automatically reaching for the gun on the
bedside table. Pushing at sheets, she climbed out.
Her back ached, her belly weighing heavily on fa-
tigued muscles. She hadn't changed from her
clothes. If anything happened, she wanted to be
ready. She never wanted to live through the ag-
ony and fear of being dragged out of a dead sleep
and across the floor by her hair again.

Moonlight fell through the window, reflecting
off the brass fittings on the wood stove, illuminat-
ing the orange of the couch. The *empty* couch.

Where was Alec? He'd been stretched on the
couch only an hour ago. Had she heard him moving around? Is that what had awakened her?

She slipped on her shoes and stepped slowly
toward the kitchen, the low carpet under her feet

muffling the sound of her footsteps. She held the pistol in front of her, pointing into the shadowed doorway. Waiting. Listening. Taking a deep breath, she stepped across the threshold.

The kitchen door flung open and the silhouette of a man filled the doorway. She brought the gun up, finger on the trigger.

"Laura."

She yanked the gun up. "Alec! What are—"

"I saw a car. I think it's them." He grabbed her arm, his fingers digging into her flesh as he physically turned her and walked her across the main room toward the porch.

She tried to think. She had their cash safely wadded in her pocket. She and Alec were both holding their weapons. The food and supplies they would have to leave. "How close are they?"

"They'll be here in a minute, tops."

"Then we can't get out in the van."

He gave his head a quick shake. "Out the back. The cabin at the end of the peninsula is occupied. They've got to have a car."

Laura spun and raced to the screened porch, Alec on her heels. The branches of evergreen were all that was visible from the porch, but she didn't have to see the ground to know it was a good fifteen-foot drop to the slope below. "How are we going to get down?"

Alec grabbed a corner of the screen and yanked. The staples holding the old steel gave way, splintering from the wood.

Laura held her breath. The sound of a car engine wound through the trees.

They were already here.

Her heart slammed against her rib cage, the force trembling through her whole body.

Alec ripped enough screen loose for her to slip out. "I'll lower you as far as I can. When you hit the ground, be sure to bend your knees to absorb the impact." He offered his hand. "And protect the baby."

She tucked her gun in the back of her waistband. Throwing a leg over the porch's half wall, she grasped Alec's forearm and he grasped hers.

He looked into her eyes and, for a split second, didn't move. Then he brought his lips down on hers.

The kiss was quick, only a light brush of his lips, but its impact shuddered to her toes. Before she could think too hard about what she was doing, she heaved her other leg over. Turning to face Alec, she locked her other arm with his and slipped over the edge.

Her knees scraped wood, the surface rough even through the denim of her jeans. Placing her feet against the wood, she inched down the siding as if repelling in some sort of mountain climbing drill, careful to keep as much distance as she could between her bulging belly and the rough siding.

Please God, don't let this send me into labor.

Muscles straining, Alec leaned through the ripped screen, lowering her until his arms and upper body could stretch no farther. "That's as close as I can get you. Ready?"

"Okay."

"Bend your knees. Try to cushion the baby."

She couldn't see how close she was to the ground. It didn't matter. She could hear the pop of tires over gravel even over the thrum of her pulse. They were close. They were pulling into the cabin's driveway. "Drop me."

"Let go on three. One…two…three." He released her just as she let go of his arms.

She plummeted. Her feet hit the uneven ground hard. She bent her knees. The force shuddered up her legs. She toppled forward. Throwing her hands out in front of her, she caught herself before she landed on her belly. Sticks bit into her palms. Mud slipped like grease beneath the cover of decaying leaves and needles. She threw her weight backward, onto her haunches just in time to keep from sprawling and rolling down the slope.

"Are you okay?"

"Fine." She didn't know if it was true, but right now it didn't matter. If they stopped, they'd be dead. And their baby would be in Ivan Stanislov's hands.

She struggled to her feet. Her legs vibrated with the impact. Pine needles stuck to muddy hands and knees. She glanced up the hill. In front of the cabin, the crunch of gravel came to a halt. "Hurry."

Alec threw one leg over the edge and then the other. Twisting to face the cabin, he dropped. He hit the ground beside her. A low grunt catapulted from his lips. Stepping forward, he slipped on the mud, but kept his footing.

Laura grabbed his arm to steady him. "I think they're parked behind the van."

"This way." He grasped her hand. They started down the hill. Stepping carefully on the slick earth, they wove through trunks of pine, birch and the occasional smooth-barked hickory.

Sticks snapped under their shoes, each crack as loud as gunfire in Laura's ears. Even in the forests' deep shadow, her pink shirt glowed. Why had she chosen to wear the pink? Alec had also bought her dark-blue and purple tops. What was she thinking? She might as well be wearing a white shirt with a target painted on the belly.

Deep male voices erupted from the crest of the hill, their words undecipherable to Laura.

Russian.

Alec bit out a low curse. "They found the screen. They know how we escaped." He reached back, under his shirt, and pulled his pistol from his waistband.

Laura reached for hers as well. Her fingers touched nothing but elastic. "Oh, no."

Alec halted and spun to face her, alarm widening his eyes. "The baby?"

"My gun. These damn maternity pants. It must have slipped out of the elastic waistband when I fell. I didn't even feel it."

"It's okay. I have mine. We're fine."

She did her best to nod and keep moving. They couldn't go back. Finding a pistol on the forest floor at night would be impossible. They were down to one gun against, no doubt, a mini arsenal of weaponry.

They passed the dark, hulking shape of a neighboring cabin. Windows stared down on them like vacant eyes. If only it was later in the year, they wouldn't be so isolated. They could reach help. Or commandeer a speed boat from a neighboring pier. As it was, the cabins along this stretch of lake didn't have their piers and boat frames in the water yet. The boats were still in storage.

Their only hope was reaching the cabin at the end of the peninsula. And once they were there, finding some sort of vehicle.

As they neared the point, bushes mixed with towering tree trunks. Branches scratched her arms. Thorns of blackberry snagged her pink blouse. Laura eyed the thick brush ahead.

She pulled on Alec's arm, stopping him in his tracks. "There's no way we can get through that thicket."

"We'll go closer to the water." He mouthed the words more than said them.

Grasping tree trunks with one hand and Alec's fingers with the other, Laura inched down the steep hill. Below, the lake sparkled in the moonlight.

With each step, she held her breath, listening for the snap of twigs behind them, until her burning lungs forced her to gasp in air.

They finally reached the water's edge. Hand in hand, they hurried close to the trees. Laura moved as quickly as she dared, her belly bouncing with each step. She cupped the baby with one arm, trying to at least partially support his weight. She'd heard too many stories about physical activity and stress triggering premature labor. She could only pray it wouldn't happen to her.

A trail of lights sparkled through the trees ahead, snaking up the hill.

Alec headed straight for them.

Drawing closer, Laura could clearly see the lights framing the landscaped path ahead. They wound up to an elaborate cabin, if the monstrosity could even be classified as a cabin. The garage alone was bigger than any of the houses in their little middle-class neighborhood back in Beaver Falls. Surely whoever owned a garage like that would have it stocked with vehicles.

Alec stopped in the shadow of a copse of trees and bushes at the path's mouth. "It looks like the path is the only way up from here."

"They'll see us in the light. My pink top will glow like a neon sign."

"We'll have to run for it." His gaze dropped to her belly. "Do you think you can do that?"

"I don't have much of a choice."

"You're not feeling contractions, are you?"

Her muscles ached and twinged from strain and fatigue, but she hadn't felt anything more. Not yet. "No. I can do it. We sure can't stay here."

He looked up at the path, his profile stark in the moonlight. "Okay. Let's go."

They dashed up the stairs. Reaching the manicured area surrounding the house, they slipped into the shadows along the garage wall. Laura searched through the woods, expecting to see the hulking shadow of Sergei Komorov, to hear a gunshot, to feel a bullet biting into her flesh.

Beside her, Alec combed the forest with his gaze. He held his pistol ready in his fist, his finger resting on the trigger. With a nod of his head, he gestured to the utility door in the side of the garage. A window stared from the top part of the door. "Check it. I'll watch for them."

Laura sidled up to utility door. Shielding the glass with her hand, she peered inside.

A motorcycle occupied the first bay of the garage, its shape cloaked by a cover emblazoned with a silver Harley-Davidson logo that caught the moonlight. Beyond it was a low-slung vehicle, probably a sports car, and in the third bay, the looming shape of a king cab pickup. "There's a truck."

"Try the door."

The brass knob was cold and slick under her sweaty palm. She prayed it would turn easily. When she was a kid, no one locked their cabin. Or if they did, they kept the key in a ridiculously convenient and obvious place. She could only hope that was still the case. She gripped the knob and turned.

It moved under her hand. Catching her lower lip between her teeth, she pushed.

The door didn't budge.

Fear crashed to her toes. "There's a dead bolt. It's locked."

Chapter Eight

Alec focused on the second garage window he would break into in less than twenty-four hours. Acid roiled in his gut. He'd worked so hard, so damn hard to leave his father's world behind, to build an upstanding life, an honest life. And in mere hours he was back where he started. Breaking into houses. Stealing cars. He had no other acceptable choice.

He glanced around the yard for something he could use to break the glass. A fist-size rock at the base of the retaining wall caught his eye. He picked it up. It wasn't as big as he'd like, but if he threw it, it might be enough. Taking a deep breath, he hurled it at the window.

The rock thudded against glass, cracking it, but failing to shatter.

Alec grabbed a branch from the forest's edge. He punched the damaged glass, making a hole big enough for his hand to fit. Reaching through, he flipped the dead bolt and opened the door. He followed Laura inside and closed the door behind them.

The garage was dark, but thanks to the landscape lighting outside and the glow of the moon, he could see the dim outlines of motorcycle, lawnmower and sports car. They wound around the vehicles until they reached the truck. Laura opened the passenger door and climbed inside.

Alec circled the vehicle. Before he slipped into the driver's seat, he needed tools.

He stopped at a work bench lining one wall. Just what he needed. He opened drawers and cupboards, rifling through the contents until he located a hammer and screwdriver that would do the trick of cracking the steering column and turning the ignition. He hadn't stolen a car since his teenage years, but it wasn't a skill one forgot. Taking the tools, he opened the driver's door and climbed inside.

Suddenly light glared all around them.

Alec's heart leaped to his throat. He waited for the Russian accent.

"What do you think you're doing, hey?"

Alec turned to see a slightly built man in a bathrobe standing in the doorway leading into the house. He cradled a deer rifle in his hands, its barrel pointed at Alec.

"This isn't the way it looks."

"Oh, yeah?"

"Really. It isn't." Alec's mind raced. Bitterness flooded his mouth. He hadn't given much thought to the occupants in the house. He'd hoped they could just slip into the garage and slip out with the truck. But, of course, they couldn't. Even if the man hadn't heard them, even if he hadn't come to the garage with his rifle to investigate, Alec couldn't very well leave him here to face his father's men. Rifle or no.

There had to be a way to handle this. A way to escape his father's men without drawing an innocent person into this hell. Or getting shot in the process. He set the tools on the console between the front seats. With his hands up, he stepped out of the truck. "We need your help."

"Stop right there. I'm warning you. I've taken down plenty of deer with this rifle."

Alec stopped. The 9mm pressed into the small of his back. He didn't want to have to use it, even as a threat. Hell, the guy was just trying to protect his property. But Alec couldn't see another way out. It was only a matter of time before his father's men caught up to them. And this guy might be an avid deer hunter, but Alec would be willing to bet he wouldn't be as good at pulling the trigger on a human being.

At least he hoped not. "My wife is going into premature labor. I have to get her to a hospital. You've got to help me."

The man stared at him as if he was speaking another language.

"Look, I'll pay for whatever damage I caused. We need your help."

Inside the truck, Laura moaned. The sound was so real and full of pain, Alec nearly forgot about the rifle pointed at him and rushed to her side. "Please. It's a high-risk pregnancy. She might lose the baby." After all she'd been through in the past few days, it wasn't much of a lie.

The guy seemed to snap out of his trance. He walked cautiously toward the pickup, peering in the window. The barrel of his rifle tilted toward the floor.

Alec reached for his gun. In one motion, he was at the man's side, the muzzle of his pistol pressed against the man's temple. "Put the rifle down."

The man's mouth formed a surprised O. He opened his fingers, dropping the rifle as if it had suddenly come alive in his hands. "Don't kill me. Please."

Alec felt sick to his stomach. The poor guy didn't deserve this. None of it. "I'm not going to kill you. Believe me, I wouldn't be doing any of this if I could help it."

Judging from the way the man's body trembled, he didn't believe a word.

"Is anyone else in the house?"

"No."

"There are some bad men out there, and they're on their way here. I'm not going to hurt you, but they will. I need to know if there's anyone else they could hurt."

"No."

"And you're telling the truth?"

"My girlfriend couldn't get off work. She's not coming up until tomorrow."

"Okay. Get in." Alec gestured to the truck.

"You're kidnapping me?"

"I'm borrowing your truck and taking you somewhere safe. Now get in."

The guy nodded like one of those bobbing head dolls. He tried to follow Alec's orders, but his fingers trembled so badly, he couldn't grip the door handle.

Alec opened the door for him. "Belt yourself in. And don't try anything. My wife will be holding the gun on you, and I have to warn you, she's an excellent shot."

As soon as the man fastened his seat belt, Alec picked up the rifle, climbed behind the wheel and handed the weapons to Laura.

She sat at an angle in the front seat, watching

the poor frightened man, the pistol in her hands, the rifle at her feet.

Alec tried to swallow the taste in his mouth. No matter what he did, it seemed, he kept drawing people into this mess, sucking them into his father's world right along with him. Sally and the employees of the Blue Ox, Laura and their unborn child, and now this poor man. It was as if the evil he had thought he'd escaped was reaching out and grabbing hold of everyone he came into contact with.

He started the engine. By now his father's men would be searching the cabins along the shore. He could only hope they weren't waiting outside already. He hit the garage door opener and backed the vehicle onto the road.

There was only one way they could go on the dead end road. Back in the direction of their cabin. "Hold on. And stay low. We might have to drive through some gunfire."

A moan of animal fear echoed in the backseat.

Alec tried not to think of his passenger. He had to keep his mind sharp and on the road ahead. All their lives depended on it.

He stomped down on the accelerator. The powerful vehicle responded. The road was a curvy, one-lane affair, twisting through brush and pine trees and pocked with mailboxes.

He piloted the beast around twists and turns. Going as fast as he dared, he had to touch the brake going into the sharp curve in front of the cabin.

The shadows of two men stood in the driveway. Two men grabbing for weapons, charging the road, firing low at the truck.

The tires. They were gunning for the tires.

Alec hit the gas coming out of the curve. Tires spun. Gravel flew. The truck fishtailed and grabbed for purchase. A pop registered somewhere in Alec's mind. The pickup bumped out of the turn, the steering suddenly soft, the sensation like trying to turn a boat on water.

They'd shot out a tire.

Alec kept going, weaving through trees and around turns, the vehicle lurching to one side. They burst onto the highway. He stomped the accelerator to the floor. Reaching the first cross road, he veered off the highway. Once they piled into their car, his father's men would be right behind them, he had no doubt. He had to make his trail impossible to follow. He had to lose them before the chase began.

He took another turn. And another. Looping around. Heading back in the direction of the cabin before veering off onto another country road. Spotting two dirt ruts leading into a large stand of pines, he veered off the road. He killed the lights and followed the path framed by the towering trunks.

Deep in the forest, he stopped and threw the truck into park, leaving the engine running and the heater blasting.

A whimper sounded from the backseat. The faint scent of urine tinged the air.

Alec cringed inwardly. Once he and Laura had disappeared and started a new life, he would have to make it up to the guy. Somehow. If that was even possible. Fix his garage window, buy him a new truck. Whatever it took.

Minutes passed. No headlights approached on the road. No whooshes of passing cars filtered through the trees. Nothing. He switched off the engine. Hands bracing on the wheel, Alec allowed himself to breathe.

It was too close. Too damned close. He couldn't let them get that close again. He had to figure something out. He had to do something. But what?

The low rumble of a voice touched the still air. He followed the sound with his gaze, until he reached the dash. The radio. The volume was so low and the truck's heater so loud, he hadn't heard it until now. Reaching forward, he turned it up.

"…and at least four people have died in an explosion in a restaurant in central Wisconsin which sources say might be tied to terrorism."

Alec's heart stuttered in his chest. Terrorism. The excuse he'd used to get the customers out of the coffee shop.

Laura stared at him from the passenger seat. He could feel the force of her questions. He could almost taste her alarm.

He glanced at the man in the back seat, willing Laura to follow his eyes, to read his concern. The last thing they needed was for their passenger to tie them to the story on the radio. Right now he had no real way to identify them. But if he tied them to the news story on the radio, he would have something to tell the Beaver Falls police.

And chances are, that something would get back to Alec's father.

"According to eyewitness reports, minutes before the explosion, a man raced into businesses neighboring the Blue Ox Café in Beaver Creek and claimed to be part of a terrorist attack. Police have identified this man as Alec Martin. Anyone who has information about this man is urged to contact authorities immediately as he is considered armed and dangerous…."

He snapped off the radio. Bitterness swirled through his mind. Damn, damn, damn. Armed and dangerous? They had it wrong. All wrong.

And because of a few confused witnesses, not only was his father after them, so were the police.

He reached for the dome-light switch above his shoulder and flicked it off in preparation for opening the door. Twisting in the seat, he glanced at the man.

A pale face looked back at him from the darkness—shell-shocked eyes, but no suspicion. No sign that he connected the report of an armed and dangerous man to Alec.

Thank God for small favors. "Where's your spare?"

"In the...the back. Under the truck bed."

Alec eyed the man. It would be easiest for Laura to control him if the two of them stayed inside the vehicle. "Stay put. I'm going to change the tire. Then we'll find someplace safe to drop you off." The rest he still had to figure out.

Chapter Nine

Terrorism? Laura's heart stuttered, then launched into double time. She switched off the radio. Her mind spun as even more questions added to the mix. While Alec had told her about the deaths at the Blue Ox and the explosion that destroyed the restaurant, he hadn't mentioned anything about clearing the Cup-N-Sup and The Fashion Place. And she didn't know how terrorism fit in. The only thing that had been clear to her from the report was that not only was the Russian mob looking for them, the police were, too.

The pickup lurched, leveling and then rising in fits and starts as Alec jacked the vehicle's weight off the shredded tire.

She'd caught Alec's look, his warning not to say anything, not to give the man in the backseat reason to believe there was a connection between them and the radio report. She could only hope he hadn't picked up on the tension in the air. Forcing what she hoped was a reassuring smile, she shifted in her seat so she could see into the back.

The man looked at her as if he thought she was crazy. The pallor of his skin matched the white of his robe. He nodded in the direction of Alec's silhouette. "That's him, isn't it? Alec Martin."

She let the smile fall from her lips. "He didn't do what they said he did."

"How do you know?"

"Because I know him. He would never do something like that. He's a good man." The words were out of her mouth before she realized what she was saying. And once she'd voiced them, she knew they were true. He had betrayed her when he'd kept from her his real name, his real past, but she didn't doubt the kind of man he was. Maybe she never really had.

A tremor spread through every cell of her body and centered in her chest. Maybe *this* was what made her so angry. This is what had made her feel so hurt. Not that she didn't know Alec. Not that she feared he was some kind of stranger. But that he was the same man. The man she'd fallen in love with. The man she'd married. It was devastating that this man she'd let so close to her heart had betrayed her.

She tried to quell the tremor. She had to get her

emotions under control. She had to talk to Alec. She had to figure out what to do now that not only the Russian mob was after them, but the police as well.

She grasped the door handle. "Hang tight, okay? I'll be right back."

The man nodded, but he didn't lean back in his seat. His eyes darted around the cab. Desperate.

She hesitated. He wouldn't be desperate enough to jump her, would he? Or try to slip out and run away? She flicked the switch on the driver's door, engaging the child-proof lock on the back doors so he couldn't open them from the inside. "You'll be fine. We'll take you somewhere safe. I'm serious. Just stay in your seat. Okay?"

He nodded.

She didn't buy his acquiescence for a minute. She grabbed the rifle from the floor and held the gun up where he could see it. "If you try to climb over the seat, I'll see you from outside. Now lean back."

He slumped in the seat.

"Don't move."

He held up his hands, palms out. "I won't."

The poor guy. "It's going to be okay. I promise." She opened the door, stepped out into the cool night and slammed it behind her. Rubbing her free hand over the goose bumps rising on her arms, she circled the truck.

Alec glanced up at her as he slipped the damaged wheel from the vehicle. "What's wrong?"

Was she that easy to read? No wonder the poor man had figured out Alec was the one in the radio report. Alarm must have been written all over her face. She gestured toward the truck. "He knows."

"Great." He set the shredded tire on the ground.

"What are we going to do?"

"What can we do? We'll drop him off somewhere. Outside of town. It'll give us a head start. We'll have to ditch the truck as soon as we can."

"And steal another?"

A muscle in his cheek flinched. "If we have to."

"What are we going to do about your father's men?"

"I've been asking myself that same question."

"And?"

"I don't have an answer yet."

That's what she was afraid of. She didn't have an answer, either. But she aimed to find one that would work. Even if Alec didn't like it. "What about turning ourselves in to the police?"

"No."

"Half the police in the state must be looking for us. They're going to find us eventually. If we turn ourselves in, we'll have more control over the situation. We can explain what happened. We can convince them to look for your father's men, maybe even charge your father."

"I think you're living in a fantasy world. We have no evidence that points to my father. Nothing but our word. Considering the circumstances, that's not worth much."

"They don't have any real evidence *against* you, either."

"They have witnesses."

Witnesses who saw Alec running from the Blue Ox. Witnesses who thought he was a terrorist. "Why do they think the explosion was a terrorist attack?"

"The damn people wouldn't get out of the coffee shop. The place was going to blow any second, and they wouldn't budge when I said it was a gas leak."

"So you told them you were a terrorist?"

"I told them it was a terrorist attack."

"So they have mistaken witnesses, witnesses whose lives you saved."

"That's more evidence than we have of my father's involvement."

"What if *we* find evidence and give it to them?"

"How do you think we're going to do that? Go back to Beaver Falls and sift through rubble?"

Pain stabbed into Laura at the thought of what

that rubble represented. Her best friend. Her colleagues. Her dream.

"I'm sorry. I shouldn't have said that." He rested a hand on her shoulder and looked into her eyes.

For a moment she couldn't look away. His tone of voice, his eyes, his touch shivered though her like a tender memory, a forgotten feeling.

She shook her head. A memory was all it was. Setting her chin, she moved away from his hand. "I'm fine."

"You're sure?"

"Yes."

He watched her for a long while before he turned away. Squatting down near the tire, he replaced the lug nuts and twisted them tight. He lowered the jack until the pickup's weight rested on the tire. "We'll disappear. This time, we'll make sure no one finds us."

She balled her hands into fists. Hadn't he heard a word she'd said? "That's not going to work. Not with the police looking for us. You're the one living in fantasyland."

"We can't turn ourselves in."

"It's the only hope of surviving this."

He stretched to his full height. "Are you forgetting what happened at Conason Park?"

"I haven't forgotten. But the police don't goof

around in cases like this. If they suspect you had anything to do with the Blue Ox, they'll have every officer in the state after you. Every officer in the country, before too long. And if they believe you're armed and dangerous, they'll shoot to kill."

She raked her hand through her hair, pushing the strands back from her face. There had to be a way out of this. "We don't have to go to the Beaver Falls police. We'll go to the county sheriff."

"No."

"Who, then? The FBI?"

"And that helped so much last time."

"It bought you, what?" She calculated in her head. "Twelve years? Thirteen? It's better than what we have now."

"Back then I had evidence that he killed a man. Evidence of extortion. Evidence of money laundering. And he was *still* out in thirteen years. Now I have nothing concrete to back me up. Just my suspicion that he ordered Sergei Komorov to kill in an attempt to get to me. I doubt he'd do one day in prison. Hell, I doubt he'd even go to trial."

He was right. They had no way to prove anything. They had nothing to convince the police of what had actually happened at the Blue Ox. But that wasn't the only crime Alec's father had committed. "How did your father find you? You said the Witness Security Program has never given away the location of a witness. So how did your father know where you were?"

"Somehow, he learned the identity of the marshal in charge of my relocation. He killed him, but not before torturing him to get my whereabouts."

Torture? More death? Laura braced herself on the side of the truck. "Have the police connected that murder to your father?"

"The last I heard, the local police think his death was a simple homicide."

"Well, maybe we can convince them differently. Where did the murder take place?"

"Madison."

"Wisconsin?"

"Yes."

"And the FBI isn't involved? I thought the murder of a federal officer came under their jurisdiction."

"It does. But because Tony Griggs was retired when he died, they don't think it's tied to his position in the Marshals' Service." Alec picked up the old tire, jack and tire iron. He walked past her, carrying his burden to the back of the truck. He lifted the items over the side and dumped them in the bed. "We have even less evidence to offer in Tony Griggs's murder."

"But unlike Beaver Falls, we can go to Madison. We can nose around."

"Bigelow said the same thing."

"Who's Bigelow?"

"A reporter from New York. The *Brooklyn Chronicle.* I became friends with him during the investigation and trial thirteen years ago. He was the only reporter more interested in the truth than the sensationalism of a mob trial."

"And you've talked to him recently?"

"I called him after I heard about Tony Griggs on the news. And one other time since. He's in Madison. He thought we should talk to the detective in charge of the case. He also has a contact in the FBI."

She tried to temper the excitement zinging along her nerves. "So maybe he's onto something. Maybe he'll help us."

"I have no doubt he will. But even if we can dig up something to give the police, and even if they do arrest my father, even convict him, I'm afraid it won't change our situation."

"He'll be behind bars."

"My father has no trouble running his business from prison."

"Maybe not. But if he likes to handle personal things personally, like you said, he won't be able to get to us."

"I don't think that will stop him this time."

"Why not?"

"Our son." He looked down at her belly. His eyes misted. His lips tightened with worry.

She covered her belly with her hands. "You mean, now that he knows about our baby…"

"He won't wait another thirteen years. He'll have someone collect his grandson for him."

"How do you know that?"

"He said it in court, at his sentencing. He gave a speech about how determined he was to fill his role as my father. And, even more important, his role as grandfather, should I have children." His voice cracked, rough with agitation. "He looked straight at me when he said it. Most of the press thought it was touching, that it meant he forgave me for testifying against him. I took it for what it was."

"A threat."

"A promise." He blew out a breath, steam jetting into the cold air. "A simple conviction is not going to solve things this time. Not even for a little while."

Laura wrapped her arms around herself, around their baby. Her sinuses burned, warning of the tears welling in her eyes. This couldn't be as hopeless as it seemed. There had to be something they could do. "You said Tony Griggs was tortured, right? He would have had to have been held against his will, maybe kidnapped."

Alec nodded.

"Could that make his murder a capital crime?"

"Not in Wisconsin. There's no death penalty."

That was right. She'd been thinking of Illinois, where she had lived most of her life before moving to Beaver Falls. But still… "The federal government has the death penalty. And the murder of a federal officer in the performance of his duty is one of the crimes that qualifies. What if we can convince the Madison police and the FBI that Tony Griggs was killed because of his job? What if we can convince them to charge him in federal court with capital murder?"

Alec nodded slowly. "It would take a long time and a lot of appeals before he would get the lethal injection."

He was right. It would take years. But there were no other options. "It's nowhere near a perfect solution, but at least it's something."

"You're right. At least it's worth a try." His words were bleak, but his voice resonated, warm with hope. Hope that blossomed in her own heart, too.

She raised a hand, wanting to touch him, to connect with him. To know he was in this with her. That they would make this work together. She caught herself before her fingers touched his sleeve.

Their plan was something they could do. Period. Something that might have a chance of changing their bleak future. But it didn't change anything about their current situation. A situation

Alec's lies had put her in—put their baby in. And even if it had changed things, she couldn't let herself touch him, connect with him, even if she wanted to. He had let her down. Destroyed her trust. Broken her heart. And she couldn't forgive him for that. She couldn't *allow* herself to forgive him.

She let her hand fall to her side. "We'd better take this poor man somewhere safe and get out of here while we have the chance."

ALEC PRESSED the lock button on the pickup's remote, tossed it onto the floor of the vehicle next to the rifle and slammed the door. He was grateful to leave the truck behind. They'd held on to it too long already by driving it the nearly four hour trip to Madison. By this time, the owner had long since walked the few miles from the spot they'd left him to the police station. Every law enforcement agency in the state was probably looking for the vehicle.

Spinning on his heel, he started across the Dane County Airport's long-term parking lot toward the spot where he'd dropped off Laura.

Even across the lot, he could see her standing in front of the exit door. Dried mud still clung to her jeans. Arms wrapped around her belly, she leaned back on her hips, balancing the baby's extra weight in the classic stance of a pregnant woman. Even tired beyond endurance, she was so beautiful his chest grew tight looking at her.

And she was full of surprises. After they'd heard the police were searching for him, he'd expected her to want to get away from him as badly as the man he'd forced into the truck had. But not Laura. Instead she'd tried to take control as she had always done in her life. She struggled to find a solution. And not for one minute had she doubted him.

And while they'd hashed out what they were going to do next, he'd felt a thread of connection between them he thought he'd never feel again. Fragile, but still intact. And it had rekindled hope he'd feared dead.

He crossed the traffic lanes in front of the terminal building and stepped onto the curb beside Laura.

She shifted and placed one hand on the small of her back.

"Contraction?"

"I'm just tired."

A wave of gratitude swept over him. So far they had dodged a bullet as far as Laura's health was concerned. He had to get her some food and a place to sleep. Then they would be ready to put their plan in motion. Now that they had a plan.

The first thing they had to do was get downtown

without attracting attention. "We need to grab a cab."

"How about a bus?" She pointed to the early-morning traffic filtering into the airport entrance. A Madison Metro bus roared toward them. And just behind it was a police car.

Spotting it as well, Laura gave him a pointed look. "We have to stay calm, relaxed. We'll just get on the bus and everything will be fine."

He dragged in a breath. He hadn't wanted to tell Laura, but he'd never been comfortable around cops. He'd always sensed they pegged him as a crook, a thug, even after he'd left his father's world. Now that he really was on their wanted list, his unease had grown into full-blown anxiety. "Money, for the fare."

"I have it." She dipped her hand into her pocket.

The bus rumbled to a stop in a wave of exhaust. Breaks squeaked. Behind it, the squad car sidled up to the curb.

Alec's pulse thumped in his ears.

The bus door's hydraulics hissed. It swung open in sync with the cop's car door.

Alec stood to the side, letting Laura climb the bus steps first. He immediately wished he hadn't. The Makarov pistol tucked in the waistband of his jeans pressed into his spine. Did the Henley he wore cover it? Or was the gun's outline visible?

Heat flushed through him. Sweat broke out on his palms. Why hadn't he bought a sweatshirt? A sweatshirt's bulk would do a better job of hiding the pistol's bulge—a shape guaranteed to catch any cop's attention.

The cop climbed from his vehicle and circled, slipping between his car's hood and the bumper of the bus.

Alec angled his body, keeping the gun hidden from his line of sight. He could only pray the police hadn't circulated his picture, that the cop didn't recognize his face.

In front of him, Laura climbed onto the bus. One step, then the next. She paused to pay the fare.

The officer stepped onto the curb.

Alec forced himself to breathe, to stay calm. For the few seconds it would take to climb onto the bus, the shape of the gun would be in plain view.

The cop's shoes clicked on the sidewalk.

Laura finished paying the fare, and moved down the bus aisle.

Alec tensed. He would have to make it fast. And hope for some luck.

He bounded up the steps. One. Then the next. And the next. He reached the top and turned down the bus aisle.

Movement registered in his periphery vision. Only a few feet away, the cop stepped even with the doorway.

Alec focused ahead. His father had always told him never to show fear, that any cop or mobster could smell it in the air like a bad odor.

He sure as hell hoped he hadn't given the cop a scent to follow.

Skipping the bank of side-facing seats, he sat next to Laura in the first row of seats that faced forward. The gun pressed into his spine. He looked to the front of the bus just as the cop's head appeared.

The officer walked slowly up the stairs. He reached the top and stopped. His gaze rested on the bus's only occupants. Alec and Laura.

Blood rushed in Alec's ears. He forced his lips to quirk upward in a slight smile of acknowledgment.

The cop took a step toward them.

Laura laughed. She grabbed Alec's hand and pressed it to her abdomen.

Confused, Alec looked into her eyes, expecting to see alarm, expecting to see fear.

He saw love. Bright, beaming love. "Did you feel that, honey?" She giggled again, the sound bright and carefree.

Alec couldn't answer. He just stared. He didn't feel any movement under his palm. But his chest tightened at the look in her eyes. The loving, happy look he'd never imagined he'd see again.

"Oh, he kicked again! Did you feel it that time?"

Alec tried to swallow the thickness in his throat. After they'd heard the radio report, he'd sensed something between them. Something real. Hopeful. *This* was acting. And recognizing this look of love was fake—that she'd *had* to fake it—rasped into his heart like a rusty hacksaw.

At the head of the bus, the cop turned and descended the steps.

"That was close." The smile faded from Laura's lips. "I was worried he might be looking for a man with a pregnant wife, but I couldn't exactly hide it. Not after he saw me waiting for the bus."

"You did the right thing. Your acting was so believable I bought it myself for a moment."

Exhaling a sigh of relief, she turned away from him and looked out the bus window.

The door hissed closed. The bus rumbled into the traffic lane. And Alec mulled over all he'd once had.

And all he'd never have again.

Chapter Ten

Alec splashed cold water on his face. The tap gave off a metallic smell of a little-used faucet, but the cool, refreshing splash felt so good he hardly noticed. The little motel might not be the Ritz, but at least it was a place to sleep. And as a result of the convoluted trail they'd created with a combination of walking and bus transfers, it was a place neither his father's men nor the police could find them.

Blotting his face with a towel, he threw the white terry cloth over his shoulder and stepped out into the room.

Laura curled on her side on one of the double beds, still fully clothed. She'd peeled back the bedspread, blanket and sheets, but had stopped there, as if the task of drawing the sheet and blanket over her had been one effort too much. Her eyes were closed, her lashes thick half-moons on pale cheeks. Her breathing rose and fell in an even rhythm.

He ached to join her, to spoon her body and sleep with her safe in his arms. Clearly an impossible dream. He crossed the room and pulled the blanket up to her shoulders. If only he could make things right with her. He'd do anything to make things right.

He pulled out his cell phone and punched in Bigelow's cell phone number.

After two rings the newspaperman answered in a sharp voice. "Yeah?"

"Late lunch. I choose the place, you pick up the check."

"Nika. You're here? In Madison?"

"Give us six hours." He glanced at Laura. It wasn't nearly enough time to erase the fatigue lining her face, but it was all they could afford to spare.

"You brought your wife?"

Alec turned away from Laura and fingered the Madison Metro schedules he'd stuffed into his pocket during their bus travels. "There's a diner in Middleton. Hubbard Street. Meet us there. Two o'clock."

"So the book is on?"

"I don't know about that. I don't want to remember what my father did, then or now. I sure as hell don't want to talk about it."

"You don't have to make your decision right away. We'll talk it over. It will be good to see you again, Nika."

Alec thought about telling Bigelow his new name. He hated answering to the name Nika. Worse, he was starting to get used to it again, an abhorrent thought. But with Alec Martin wanted for multiple murders and by this time, kidnapping and car theft, too, it might be a good idea to keep his new name quiet. Even from Bigelow. "Come alone. And don't be late." He turned his phone off to conserve the batteries and snapped it shut.

"What exactly happened with your father?"

He turned to look at Laura.

She met his eyes, her head still resting on the pillow. "What made you decide to go to the FBI?"

"I told you. He killed a man."

"There's more to it than that. I can feel it. And I deserve to know."

A hum rose in Alec's ears. Telling Laura about that day was the last thing he'd choose. He didn't want to tie himself to Ivan Stanislov any more than he already was, especially not in her eyes. But if giving her the whole truth now would make up for his past distortions in any small measure, he would do it. He owed her. "It happened on my eighteenth birthday. My father took me to visit a jeweler in Manhattan, on Diamond Row. I thought he was going to buy me a birthday gift. A watch or something." He stopped. The hum in his head, the heaviness in his chest was unbearable.

"But he didn't buy you a watch?"

"The owner had given my father's mistress a necklace. Nothing expensive, just a simple gold chain. He probably meant it as a show of respect, but my father didn't see it that way. The guy hadn't asked my father's permission to give her the gift. To Ivan Stanislov, that's a personal betrayal."

Laura lay perfectly still. She watched him with a penetrating stare, as if willing him to continue.

"He beat the jeweler with a baseball bat. Sergei was standing right behind him, but my old man did the beating himself. He bragged that he always took care of personal matters personally. It's all about honor, he liked to say. Honor. What a damn joke."

He had only to close his eyes, and he'd be back there. Seeing. Smelling. Hearing. "Do you know what kind of sound a wood bat makes hitting flesh? Breaking bone?"

Laura's throat moved, as if she was trying to swallow but couldn't. But she didn't turn away. She didn't stop him.

"I'll never forget the sound. You can't hear the bones breaking, not really. It's just a dull thunk, like pounding a dead side of beef. Like nothing. It doesn't make sense that something so brutal sounds like nothing." He sometimes heard the sound in dreams. The simple thunk. It turned his stomach.

He shook his head, still trying to make sense out of all of it and coming up short. "But the screams. The screams are different." He heard those in his dreams too.

"What did you do?" Her voice came out a whisper.

"I just stood there and watched. I couldn't turn away. I couldn't move. I knew my father's money came from breaking the law, swindling the state out of gas taxes, defrauding insurance companies. Those scams seemed harmless to me back then, like victimless crimes. But this—" He shook his head. The brutality. The depravity. The memory of it still jarred him to his bones. "When the guy ran out of screams, my father handed the bat to me."

She sucked in a breath. "You didn't—"

"Beat him?" He winced. It was the reason he hadn't wanted to tell her, the fear she would think he was capable of such brutality. That she would believe since he was his father's son, he must be like him. "I threw the bat down and left. But it didn't matter. It was already too late. The guy was dead. I know he was. His body was found the next morning. They made it look like a robbery gone bad."

"And that's when you went to the FBI?"

He nodded. "I left that life and didn't look back."

Her arm moved under the blanket. Her hand rested on the baby. "What about your mother? Did you leave your mother, too?"

His heart constricted, her question wringing the blood from it. He'd tried not to think of his mother. He never spoke about her. And seeing Laura in bed, caressing her belly, made the pain even sharper. And no matter how he wanted to, it was a pain he couldn't ignore. "I had to cut all ties. All contact. The last time I saw her was when I took the witness stand in my father's trial. She looked so sad. So old. She died a year later. She died totally alone."

Laura watched him, saying nothing.

Only the whoosh of cars racing by on the highway outside cut the silence. Only the relief of putting his past in the open lessened the hurt twisting in his chest. The regret aching in his bones.

He forced his feet to carry him back into the bathroom. Leaning on the cold marble countertop, he stared at himself in the mirror. Dark circles girded gray eyes. Creases carved into his forehead. Stress bound his jaw.

He was the one who looked sad now. He was the one who looked old.

When he'd entered the witness security program, he had forbidden himself from thinking about any of the people he'd known in the past, including his mother. It was just too painful otherwise. He'd told himself Nika Stanislov was dead. That Alec Martin was a different person with a different life and different friends. The truth was, Alec had no real life, no friends, no memories. Alec hadn't even been a person until he'd met Laura.

And he couldn't help wondering if he would fade back to nothingness without her.

LAURA WAS FAMISHED by the time they walked into the Hubbard Street Diner. Scents of eggs and coffee swirled around her, making her stomach growl so hard she thought she'd be sick. Delicious-looking pies, cheesecakes and muffins caught her attention from the glass showcase as they entered, and it was all she could do to keep herself from diving over the case and digging in.

She followed Alec into the restaurant. She didn't know if he'd gotten any sleep, but she was grateful to see him holding his shoulders strong and square as he wove through tables and around chairs. She wanted to see him strong. Not vulnerable. Not like he'd been this morning.

She should never have asked him about his

past. She should have known better. She'd pre-
pared to stomach his father's brutality. She'd
braced herself for that. But she hadn't counted on
seeing Alec's pain so vividly etched on his face.
She hadn't counted on hearing how his decision
to do the right thing had destroyed his mother.
She hadn't counted on feeling for him, caring for
him.

And she couldn't let it happen again.

Alec stopped at a booth in front of a curved
wall of glass block. The man behind the table
grinned at him. Crow's-feet creased freckled skin,
fanning out from eyes that didn't seem to miss a
single detail. "Nika." He scooched out of the
booth and stood. White tufts of hair topped his
head, adding three inches to his height. He
thumped Alec on the back, then he cocked his
head in Laura's direction. He offered her his hand.
"It's an honor meeting you, Mrs. Stanislov."

Her mind balked at the name. "Call me Laura."
She shook his offered hand.

"Laura. A beautiful name for a beautiful lady."

She did her best not to roll her eyes.

"Too much, huh?"

"I'd say." She released his hand, unable to hide
her smile.

An answering smile spread over the man's
thick lips. "My mother always said I was born too

late, that I should have lived in a more courtly age."

Alec motioned Laura into the booth and shot Wayne Bigelow a frown that barely concealed his grin. "You can save your courtliness for picking up the check."

Laura slid into the booth, leaving the men to face off on either side.

The men took their seats just as the waitress appeared at the table. They placed their orders. Once the waitress had gone, Wayne focused on Alec. "I guess I owe you double congratulations. Not only a wife but a baby."

Alec nodded. Although he seemed genuinely glad to see his friend, tension pinched the space between his brows and jiggled his leg under the table. He glanced around the restaurant as if expecting his father's men or the police to burst in any moment. "We've come up with a plan about how to handle my father, Wayne, and we're hoping you can help."

"Of course I'll help. What's your plan?"

They paused as the waitress plopped coffee cups in front of them. She placed two insulated pots on the table, as well. Caffeinated for Wayne and Alec, and decaf for Laura. As she walked away, Alec skewered Bigelow with a no-nonsense look. "We want to find a way to convince the police to turn over the Griggs case to the FBI."

"Because Griggs was a U.S. marshal."

"Right. He wouldn't have been killed except for his job."

"We want Ivan Stanislov prosecuted for a capital offense," Laura added.

"Of course. Brilliant. Wisconsin doesn't have the death penalty, but the feds do." Elbows on table, Wayne Bigelow leaned forward and wrapped long fingers around his coffee cup. "So how do I fit in?"

"We need to dig up some kind of evidence. Something that shows my father's involvement in Tony Griggs's death beyond my say-so. Have you talked with Griggs's wife?"

"Ah, yes. The widow Griggs. Quite a piece of work."

Laura tried to quell the hope skipping through her veins. Getting too hopeful this early would only lead to a crash. Especially considering the steep odds they were facing. "Can you introduce us? Convince her to talk to us?"

Wayne nodded, his white curls bobbing. "I think I can come up with something. For you." He gave her a wink and a smile.

Alec shifted in his seat. "There's more."

Bigelow turned his attention back to Alec. "Shoot."

"We need a car."

"You can rent one—"

"We don't want to rent one. We just want to borrow yours."

Wayne arched bushy brows.

"I don't want to go into my reasons right now."

Wayne tilted his head to one side, as if weighing the decision. Pursing his lips, he gave a nod. "The car is yours. No accidents, hear?"

"I'll do my best."

"You're not making me feel good about this, Nika."

"Sorry." Alec gave him a smile, but the muscles under the grin remained tense.

Laura tried not to notice, focusing instead on Bigelow. "We also need you to help us contact the police detective in charge of the Griggs case."

Bigelow nodded while sipping his coffee. His pronounced Adam's apple bobbed as he swallowed. "Too bad my FBI contact went back to New York. You could have dealt with him directly, cut out the middle man."

"Can you call him?" Laura asked.

"I'll try. Sometimes it takes a bit to reach him, though. His name is Callahan. He's part of the FBI's Russian Organized Crime Unit. A busy man."

Alec lifted his coffee cup, then set it down without taking a sip. "You said you thought this detective was trustworthy."

"Mylinski. He's a detective for the county. Good man. I can set up a meeting with him while I'm trying to reach Callahan."

"Don't bother."

Bigelow canted his head at Alec in an unspoken question.

"I don't want him to know about us ahead of time."

"A surprise meeting?"

"Yes. Do you know where he lives?"

"I can find out. Why the secrecy?"

"I'll tell you later. You can put it in your book."

Bigelow beamed. "You've rethought the book? Wonderful."

Laura wasn't following. "Book?"

Bigelow looked from Alec to Laura and back again. "Should I give you two a moment?"

Alec held up a hand. He turned to Laura. "Bigelow is writing a book about the Russian Mafia. He wants my story."

Out of all the things she imagined him saying, she never saw this coming. Not after his obvious pain when telling her his story this morning. He'd said he knew Bigelow would help them, that they could trade favors. But Laura hadn't guessed Alec would agree to pay such a steep price. She leaned toward him. "Are you sure you want everything you went through in a book?"

A muscle clenched along his jaw. "It's only fair."

To anyone else, his voice probably sounded strong and certain. Only she could detect the vulnerability under the words. It slashed at her heart like a sharp blade.

She touched his arm before she caught herself. Oh, God. This was just what she was worried about. She couldn't let herself feel for him. From there it was just a short step down the path to trusting. To loving. A path she couldn't take, *wouldn't* take. Not again.

She dropped her hand in her lap. "Fine, Alec. It's your decision."

"Alec?" Wayne looked confused for a moment. Then he chuckled. "Ahh, Nika. I forgot you have a different name, my friend."

Alec offered him another tense smile.

Wayne looked at Alec a little harder. "Your name wouldn't be Alec Martin, would it?"

Alec said nothing.

A weight thudded into Laura's stomach.

"You're the one police all over the state are looking for? The one that caused the restaurant explosion?"

Laura sat forward. "Alec didn't cause anything. His father did."

Wayne nodded, but his jocular manner was clearly long gone, replaced by an air of worry. "Of course Ivan did it. But that's not what the police believe. They're after your husband for murder. And by lending you my car and doing you favors, I might be buying myself a charge of my own. 'Accessory after the fact.'"

Laura's stomach lurched. They'd come here to enlist an ally. They might leave creating a police informant.

Alec didn't seem shaken. "It will be worth it, Bigelow. I'll make it worth it to you. Remember the book."

"A publishing deal won't do me a lot of good in prison."

Alec fixed him with a hard look. "All right. No book."

Bigelow scrubbed a hand across his face. "Okay, okay. I'll see what I can do."

Alec nodded. Confident.

Laura wasn't so sure. Not about her empathy for Alec, not about trusting Bigelow, and as she watched the waitress weave toward their table with a big tray of food, she didn't even know if she could eat.

Chapter Eleven

Alec craned his neck to look up at the three-story house complete with turrets on Madison's far west side. The late-afternoon sun slanted from the west, catching the stained-glass windows surrounding the entrance and turning the reds and oranges to brilliant fire.

He'd had to use a little strong arm to convince Bigelow to agree to help them. And now that they were committed, unease crept over him like a damp chill. He had a bad feeling about this. A very bad feeling. "Does this seem to you to be the kind of place a retired U.S. marshal could afford?" He held open the door of Bigelow's rental car and offered Laura his hand.

She took it, staring at the house as she climbed from the car. "Maybe his wife has money."

"Or maybe my father didn't need to kill him to

get my location. Maybe he had been buying information like that from Griggs for a long time."

"The fact that a law enforcement officer has money doesn't necessarily mean he's crooked."

"In my father's world, it usually does."

"So if your father bought Tony Griggs off, who killed him?"

"The more important question isn't who killed him, but what the hell are we going to do if my father *didn't*."

Laura's shoulders slumped at the question. "Let's not jump to conclusions. Let's just go in and talk to this woman, find what we need to find."

He nodded and started up the cobblestone sidewalk. She was right. Jumping to conclusions wouldn't get them anywhere. They needed specifics, details about Tony Griggs's life and money and his death. If the evidence they needed to tie the murder to his father was there, they'd find it.

Reaching the elaborate entrance, he jabbed the bell.

Chimes echoed and reverberated as if the house was as big and empty as a damned cavern.

"May I help you?"

Alec and Laura spun around.

A petite woman peered at them around tall bushes at the corner of the house. A visor fitted over gray hair, she squinted into the afternoon sunlight. Hands covered by brightly flowered gloves gripped a garden trowel.

"Mrs. Griggs?" Alec asked.

"Yes?"

"We need to ask you some questions about your husband."

Lipsticked lips drooped in a frown. "I've answered all the questions I'm going to. You people haven't left me alone for one minute in the past two days."

"We aren't the police."

"Who are you, then?"

"Wayne Bigelow sent us. He's a reporter for the *Brooklyn Chronicle?* He said he'd spoken to you?"

"You're the true crime writers."

So that's the story Wayne had decided to use. Interesting. "Yes. Do you have a moment?"

"Sure." She was glowing now. Strange how the promise of fame, regardless of ghoulish circumstances, could turn people's heads. Even a grieving widow's. "I just love Ann Rule's books."

Laura smiled at the woman and nodded. "Yes, she's wonderful."

"Do you know her?"

"I'm afraid not." Laura glanced at Alec and back to Mrs. Griggs. "Would it be possible to see your house?"

"Oh, you want to see where I found him?"

"You found him?"

"He was in the basement. On the pool table. I'm afraid the police took the table, though." She pulled the gloves off manicured fingers, her lips tight and troubled.

The first sign of distress Alec had noticed coming from Mrs. Griggs, and it was brought on not by her husband's murder, but by the police taking a doubtlessly blood-soaked pool table for evidence. Clearly this woman had her priorities a bit skewed.

"Maybe you can get copies of the crime photos from the police."

Not in any reality Alec was aware of, but he played along. "I'm sure that won't be a problem." He glanced at Laura.

Judging from her expression, she was as horrified by their "grieving" widow as he was. At least they didn't have to worry about tiptoeing around this woman's feelings.

Mrs. Griggs opened the front door and led them into the arching foyer. Decorated in gray marble and rich woods, the interior of the mansion was as imposing as the exterior. And as expensive looking. The uneasy feeling that had crept up his spine when they'd pulled up to the house assaulted him with a vengeance. "You have a beautiful home."

"Thank you. Tony was very lucky with money."

Alec tried to infuse a nonchalant lilt into his voice. "Oh, really? How is that?"

"He made some great investments. That's how we could retire early."

Investments? Like trading information for money with a mobster? "What kind of investments did he make?"

She looked at him, her wrinkle-free face troubled. "Are you implying something about my husband's money? What are you trying to say?"

Alec considered his answer. Mrs. Griggs might not be fazed by her husband's death, but apparently she *was* sensitive about where he had gotten his money. "I was just wondering if money might be involved in his death."

She dismissed his statement with a wave of her hand. "Certainly not. But I know where you're going with this. The same place the police want to go. But I'll tell you right now, Tony didn't get his money illegally. And no one has a claim on it but me."

So that was this woman's angle. Money. And fame, of course. The two went hand in hand. He should have known. "I didn't mean to suggest your husband did anything illegal."

"Good. Because if that's what you're going to write, I'm not going to go any further with this interview."

So much for finding out more from Mrs. Griggs about the money angle. He'd better stick to the murder, or he and Laura were going to get kicked out before any of their questions were answered. He glanced at Laura.

Reading his plea for help, she pulled the microcassette recorder Wayne had lent them from her pocket. "Do you mind if I turn this on?"

Mrs. Griggs actually brightened at the sight of the recorder. "Oh, go ahead. I want you to get the story right, of course. My name is spelled D-o-r-o-t-h-i. With an *i*. Got that?"

"You bet." Laura gave her a smile. "Now where did you say you found Mr. Griggs?"

"This way." Dorothi Griggs led them to a sweeping staircase that curved around the far wall of the foyer. One section of steps led to the upper level, one to the lower.

They walked down the stairs, their footsteps silent on the plush carpet. The room at the base of the steps was like something from a sports lover's dream. Autographed jerseys in gilded frames lined the walls. Everything from a poker table to pinball machines scattered the room. And in the middle of it all, a big-screen television held court.

"The police let me call a cleaning crew this afternoon. They finished about an hour ago. I'm so glad you didn't have to see the way the police left it. Black powder everywhere. Dirty footprints. It was a mess."

"Great." So anything they might have learned by examining the room had been cleaned. Swept away just like any grief Dorothi might have felt. Alec focused on the woman. Her memory of what she'd seen was their only shot at learning something useful about the crime. He sure as hell hoped she hadn't wiped that clean, as well. "Just tell us what you remember."

"He was down here in our rec room. Like I said, he was on top of the pool table, tied down." She motioned to an empty spot near a bank of windows that peered into a hot tub room.

"What was he tied with?" Alec probed.

"That was kind of an interesting thing." She pointed to the tape recorder in Laura's hand. "Are you sure that thing can pick up my voice from that far away?"

Laura raised the device to within inches of Dorothi's lips.

Dorothi smiled. "Like I was saying, the way he was tied was interesting. The pool table had these spaces at the top. It was part of the design. And the murderer tied Tony's arms and legs by threading little plastic strips through the gaps and around his arms. You know those thick plastic strips you see in stores sometimes? The kind that lock and you have to cut to get loose?"

Alec knew just the kind. He thought of Sally, of the plastic strips around her wrists. And of her hands. "Dorothi, do you remember anything about Tony's hands?"

"Hands? As in the way he was tied?"

"Not just that. Was there any damage to his hands? Broken fingers?"

"Why, yes. How did you know? His fingers were purple. And kind of skewed."

"Broken."

"Yes." She leaned toward Alec and lowered her voice. "That's why the police thought it was torture at first."

And that was how he could tie the murder to Sergei Komorov and through Sergei, to his father. He glanced at Laura. All that was left was convincing the police. Before they threw him in jail for murder.

SERGEI KOMOROV wasn't a patient man. And with his head aching and face throbbing, whatever patience Sergei did have had burned hours ago.

He stared out the bug-pocked window of the truck stop and watched cars and semis whizzing by on the interstate. "You can't tell me that a red pickup truck disappeared. A vehicle that size doesn't just disappear."

Pavel sopped up runny eggs with a crust of toast and held it poised and dripping over his plate. "He dumped it. He had to. The cops would have found him by now if he was still driving the thing."

"So what did he do after he dumped it?"

"He stole another one," Pavel said and jammed the toast in his mouth.

"So are you monitoring reports of stolen cars?"

"In the whole state? He could have gone anywhere by now."

Sergei grunted. He didn't need the reminder. "So look everywhere. You're supposed to be the computer genius."

Sergei watched Pavel chew. The kid was annoying, but Sergei had to admit he didn't hate him personally as much as he hated what Pavel stood for. The new mobster, the future of the Russian Mafiya. His kind preferred computers to guns, complicated stock scams to old-fashioned extortion. And while anything that made money was fine by Sergei, he didn't like the idea of kids like Pavel horning in on his warm spot. The spot he'd earned and felt was steadily slipping away.

Especially now that he'd lost Nika twice.

"You done stuffing your damn face? I don't think Nika is standing around waiting for you."

Pavel gave him a hard look. He pushed his chair back and stood. "I'll be in the car."

The little prick. "Good."

The kid stalked away.

Sergei smiled. He liked treating the wunderkind like crap. It made him feel better. Less like the world was changing too fast and he'd never be able to catch up. Less like he was a dinosaur. More like he still had the power he'd had before Ivan's *musor* son had sent him away.

The ringing of his cell phone cut through the clattering dishes and silverware. Ivan. Sergei could only hope that Ivan's source had given him something. That the call didn't mean Ivan had lost patience, that heads were about to roll. Namely his.

Sergei flipped open the phone and held it to his ear. "Ivan?"

"I have an address for you."

Chapter Twelve

Narrowing her eyes, Laura searched for the address Wayne Bigelow had given them as Alec drove slowly down the quiet residential streets of Madison's near west side. Bigelow was right about the neighborhood where Detective Mylinski lived. Small, boxy starter homes lined shady streets. Most houses were lucky to have a one-car garage. And she doubted any of those garages had anything fancier than an economy car inside. It was not the type of place someone with money was likely to live. Even Alec didn't have reason to believe Al Mylinski was on the take.

She spotted the house number on the mailbox of a green house snuggled into a wooded corner lot. The windows were dark. No one home. "There it is."

"Got it." Alec drove a block from the house before pulling to the curb, shifting into Park and switching off the ignition. He reached under the seat and pulled out the Mak.

"You can't bring the gun."

"I'm not going to leave it here."

She shook her head. He wasn't listening. "If you act like a criminal, this Detective Mylinski is going to peg us as criminals. He's not going to believe a word we say."

Alec's lips curved into a one-sided frown. But he didn't pull the gun out of his waistband.

"Growing up with your father, you know how criminals think. I know how cops think, Alec. You're going to have to trust me on this. If you're armed, we don't stand a chance."

"Okay. I'll stash the gun in the bushes near the house. Somewhere we can reach it."

He hadn't added "in case something goes wrong." But Laura could feel the sentiment hanging in the air, ominous as gathering thunder clouds. Hiding the pistol near the house might not be the perfect solution, but she had to admit she didn't want to be without a weapon, either. "Fair enough."

Jumping out of his own door, he circled the car and offered Laura his hand.

She hesitated. She didn't want to touch him, even to let him help her out of the low-slung car. Every touch, every look lapped at her anger like water against sandbags. And she couldn't afford to let the dam break.

She pushed herself out of the car on her own. "The detective will be home anytime. We'd better go."

It didn't take long to walk the three blocks to the little green ranch-style house. The front of the house was wooded with plenty of trees and bushes. Good. Laura felt better with a little cover. Between the bushes and the long shadows of early evening, they could stay out of view until the detective reached the house. Then they'd have to do their best to convince him of their story.

As promised, Alec hid the gun at the base of one of the yews on the corner of the hedge that lined the house's foundation like table skirting. Standing to the side of the cement stoop, they waited for the detective to return.

They didn't have to wait long. Twenty minutes later a beat-up brown car swept into the driveway and stopped in front of the garage. A man stepped from the car. Heavy-set and balding, he wore one of the worst suits Laura had ever seen. Definitely an honest cop.

Laura hefted herself onto her feet. Stepping off the stoop, she walked down the sidewalk to meet him, her gait the disarming waddle of a pregnant woman. She usually hated the waddle she'd developed over the past few weeks or so, especially how pronounced it became whenever she got tired. But now she was grateful. It was hard for anyone to be too suspicious of a pregnant woman. And right now she'd embrace anything that would lend their story more credibility.

As the detective drew closer, Laura could make out the tell-tale bulge of a shoulder holster under his limp suit coat. He offered her a smile as she approached. A smile that didn't quite reach sharp hazel eyes.

"Detective Al Mylinski?" Laura said.

He came to a stop several feet away, his right foot slightly behind his left, protecting his gun side. "What can I do you for?"

"We need to talk."

"Oh? About what?"

Alec stepped up behind Laura. "Tony Griggs."

If the detective was surprised, he didn't show it. "What do you have for me?"

"I know who killed him," Alec said.

The detective didn't react. No raising of eyebrows. No stepping forward. No nothing. "And?"

"And why."

"Are you going to share this revelation with me?"

"He was killed because of a case he handled thirteen years ago. When he was with the U.S. Marshal Service."

"Hmm." A frown shifted over the detective's features. He dipped his hand in his pocket.

Laura could feel Alec tense beside her, as if he was about to bolt.

The detective drew out a handful of colorful candy. He thrust his cupped palm toward them. "Want one?"

Laura's stomach tried to do a flip. "No, thank you."

Shrugging, Detective Mylinski unwrapped a candy and popped it into his mouth. The scent of lemon tinged the air. "So are you going to tell me who killed Tony Griggs, or are we just going to spend some quality time staring at each other?"

"My father. Or rather my father's man, Sergei Komorov."

The detective's eyebrows arched toward his balding pate. "Okay, I'll bite. Who's your father?"

"Ivan Stanislov."

"Russian, eh. Mob?"

"Yeah."

His cheeks puckered as he sucked his candy. "I guess that would explain the feds' interest in this case. So why do you think your father's man is my murderer?"

"Sergei has a thing for breaking fingers. And faces."

"And how do you know Tony Griggs's fingers were broken?"

"That's not important."

"Actually it is."

Laura stepped forward, purposely coming between Alec and the detective. "We talked to his widow. She told us his fingers were broken when she found him."

Alec adjusted his position so he once again had a straight shot at the detective. "Komorov also likes to use those nylon strips for binding hands."

"Sounds like Widow Griggs was a fountain of information."

"She was helpful."

Detective Mylinski used his tongue to click the lemon candy against his teeth while he studied them. "So why are you all fired up to sic the FBI on your father? What did he do? Write you out of the will?"

Alec gritted his teeth.

"Alec testified against him thirteen years ago," Laura explained in an even voice. "When he went to prison, Alec went into the Witness Security Program."

"Go on."

"Ivan Stanislov was recently released. He sent men after us. To kill us."

Mylinski turned those eyes back on Alec. "And let me guess, Tony Griggs was in charge of your relocation."

He nodded. "The day after Tony Griggs's death, my father's men showed up at Laura's restaurant."

"Interesting timing, all right." Mylinski watched them as if he could read every nuance of body language, every quickened breath and racing beat of their pulses. "Answer me a question, will you?"

"If I can," Alec answered.

Mylinski zeroed in on Alec. "I was just wondering when you were going to explain exactly what happened at Mrs. Martin's restaurant. You are Alec Martin, aren't you?"

Oxygen seized in Laura's chest. Next to her, she could almost feel Alec bristle. She tried to catch his attention. He had to play this cool. She willed him to look at her.

He glanced at her and then back to Mylinski. "My father's men—Sergei Komorov and others—tried to get to Laura. And if you care to look, you'll find his trademarks up there, too."

Images of Sally mixed with Dorothi Griggs's description of how she'd found her husband, was making Laura dizzy, making her sick. She watched Mylinski's face. He had to believe them.

He had to help. If he didn't, she didn't know where they would turn.

Mylinski sucked on his candy while he studied Alec. "Why did you risk coming here tonight? You had to know I can't just let you walk away."

"In my experience, honest cops are hard to find. I heard you're an honest cop."

"Have you run into some that aren't so honest?"

"Yes. In Beaver Falls."

"Who?"

"I don't know. I just know things aren't as they should be up there. We don't want to go back."

Laura's pulse pounded a tattoo in her ears. She strained to hear over the beat. He had to help them. "Alec didn't do what they are saying. He didn't do anything wrong."

Mylinski looked from her to Alec. "Will you agree to cooperate with the investigation up there? Help us get to the truth?"

"As long as there's no jail time. And as long as we don't get sent back."

Mylinski watched them for what felt like hours. Finally he nodded. "I'll give Callahan a holler. In the meantime, I'll see what I can do to keep you here in Madison."

Laura let out a relieved breath. For the first time since this nightmare started, it seemed as if there might be a way out. That they weren't all alone. That there might be a reason to hope.

A gun shot blasted through the quiet neighborhood.

Chapter Thirteen

Fear seized Laura a split second before Alec plowed into her, pushing her into the thick bushes near the corner of the house. He flattened himself on top of her, shielding her with his body. Her belly pressed against the hard planes of his chest, compacting her lungs and knocking the air out of her.

Another shot punctured the air.

Laura's heart stopped at the sound, then started beating so hard, she thought she'd be sick.

The mobsters had found them.

Her mind spun with helplessness. She was panting, but her lungs didn't seem to be taking in enough air. She felt like she was drowning. "I can't breathe."

Alec shifted his weight off her. Grabbing her arm, he pulled her deeper into the space between the hedge of yews and the house.

She gasped.

"Slower. You're hyperventilating."

She tried to breathe slower, but she still felt as if she was drowning, in panic, in visceral fear.

"I can't believe he would sell us out. How could he have sold us out?"

"Who?"

"Bigelow." Alec spat the name, as if it tasted bitter on his tongue. "I just can't believe he'd do it. I never saw it coming."

"Maybe it wasn't him. Maybe they found out where we were some other way."

"He's the only one who knew we were here." Pain and betrayal laced his words. After all the precautions he'd taken, he'd ended up trusting someone on his father's payroll, anyway. Someone he'd been tricked into believing was an old friend. "Oh, hell."

She tried to sit up, tried to shift so she could see what Alec was exclaiming about. Through the green-needled bushes, she spotted Detective Mylinski on the ground near the sidewalk, his back to a small clump of birches. The slender white trunks did little to afford him cover.

Why didn't he get out of there? The yard was filled with many bushes and trees denser than those birches. Why didn't he get somewhere that would afford him more cover?

He glanced in her direction. His face was red, bald head sweaty. Gritting his teeth, he reached for his gun. His jacket flapped open. Red stained his white shirt.

Blood.

Fear bubbled up inside her. "The detective. He's shot."

Alec gripped her arm. "Stay down."

She hadn't realized she'd risen to her knees. She hunkered back down next to Alec. "The detective—"

He flipped open his cell phone. "Damn."

"Battery?"

"It's dead." He dropped it on the ground. "I'm going out there. I'm going to try to reach him."

Dread squeezed down on her chest. "It's too dangerous. You could get hit, too."

"I'm not going to leave him."

"We're in a residential neighborhood. Someone had to have heard the shots. Someone will call the police."

"And even if they aren't crooked, they might be too late. Listen, I brought him into this mess. I have to make sure he's okay."

"The gun—"

"It's too far away. I'll have to go without it."

He watched the detective, the muscles surrounding his mouth and eyes flinching as if he could feel the detective's pain. He was scared for the man; that much was clear. Scared enough to risk his life.

But then, he'd risked his life for others many times in the past two days. Especially for her. As if he was responsible for his father and Sergei Komorov. As if it was his job to protect the world from their evil. "Wait just a few minutes. Help will be here soon."

"And he might be dead by then." Alec slipped around her. Poised in the space between the bushes and the cement stoop, he twisted to look at her over his shoulder, to search her eyes. "Promise me you'll stay here."

She didn't want to promise. "What if you get shot? What if you need my help?"

"Promise me. Remember our baby."

He was right. She had to think of their son. She had to keep him safe. Helplessness rose in her throat like a scream. She choked it down. "I promise."

He slipped out of the shelter of the bushes and started crawling for the detective.

"Be careful."

He nodded, but kept moving across the twenty-foot span, his body flat to the ground, arms and legs propelling him. Finally he reached the detective. Staying low, he hunched over him.

The air was still around them. No popping of gunfire. No sound of approaching footsteps. Nothing. As if the gunmen had disappeared.

But she knew that wasn't the case. It couldn't be. They wouldn't just give up. And they certainly wouldn't just disappear. Not until they got what they came for. Alec. And their son.

Panic rasped against every nerve in her body. She needed to get up, to do something. Not just wait here passively.

From this angle, Laura could see the detective's face. Teeth clamped together, his eyes squinted with pain. He gripped his side, as if holding his flesh together with his bare hands.

Alec peeled the suit coat off the detective's arms. Gathering it into a wad, he held it against Mylinski's side, helping him move his hand on top of it to hold it in place.

Alec groped under Mylinski's suit coat and pulled out his cell. He punched numbers and held the phone to his ear. "There's been a shooting. An officer has been hurt. We need an ambulance and plenty of police. Now!"

Laura concentrated on breathing slowly. In and out. In and out. They were still out there. She knew they were. Moving in. Getting closer. She couldn't just lie here. No matter what she'd promised Alec, she had to do something. The gun. She needed the gun. She could stay in the bushes and still reach the gun.

As Alec recited the address into the phone, she

started moving, crawling between house and bushes. Sharp needles clawed her cheeks and caught in her hair. White landscaping stones bit into her hands and knees. She pushed on, reaching the corner of the house. Peeking through needled branches, she spotted the Mak's dull silver gleam. She stretched out a hand to grab it.

A black boot emerged from the bushes and stepped on the gun. Brutality gleaming from hard eyes, Sergei Komorov smiled down at her, an angry scar stretching across his cheek.

"IT IS OVER, NIKA."

Sergei Komorov's rough growl ripped through Alec with the force of a bullet. He looked up from the detective's pain-pinched face, from the bloody jacket he pressed to his wound.

Sergei smiled at him from the corner of the house. The cut Alec had carved across his face with the shovel had been stitched, but the sewn edges were red and angry, transforming Sergei's flat face into a mask straight from hell. "It is time for you to come home. Face what you did."

A cold mix of fear and rage seized Alec's chest. He should have killed the bastard when he had the chance. He glanced away from Sergei, searching the bushes along the house for the shimmer of blond hair. The shadow of movement. Where was Laura?

"You are looking for your wife?" Sergei reached down into the bush in front of him—the same bush Alec had used to conceal the Mak. But when he straightened, instead of the gun in his fist, he was gripping Laura by the hair.

Alec's heart froze. He dropped the cell phone, letting it clatter to the sidewalk. He had to do something. He had to get that bastard's hands off Laura.

"My gun."

Alec looked down, in the direction of the weak whisper.

The detective stared up at him, as if willing him to understand. He clutched the bloody jacket to his chest with one hand and in the other, he held his pistol. "Take it."

Alec closed his hand around Mylinski's fist. Taking the gun from the detective's fingers, he kept it low, out of Sergei's line of sight. Slipping off the safety, he looked back to the mobster.

He couldn't see a weapon in Sergei's hand. Not a gun or a knife. But that didn't mean he wasn't armed. Sergei was always armed. Alec thought of the other man, the one who had been waiting in the car outside the house. The one who had fired at them at the cabin. No doubt he'd shot the detective while Sergei circled the house. And where was he now? Did he have Alec in his sites? Or Laura?

"I run out of patience, Nika." Sergei still held

Laura by the hair at the edge of the bushes. "You don't want to come home? That is fine. I have what Ivan wants most. A grandson. A boy to raise into the man his son never was."

"Like hell."

A flash of movement stirred the bushes. Laura's hand lashed out, aiming for Sergei's crotch.

Sergei moved to the side.

Laura's hand landed harmlessly on his thigh. But it was all the distraction Alec needed.

He leveled the gun on Sergei and fired.

The shot went wide. Alec fired again.

Sergei jumped back. Unable to pull Laura through the bushes, he released her hair and ducked around the corner of the house.

Alec fought the urge to run to Laura's side, to gather her in his arms and sweep her away from the gunfire, the danger. He couldn't give Sergei the chance to get them both. He had to keep Sergei pinned behind the house if Laura was to have a chance to get away. He fired another shot at the corner of the house. "Laura! Crawl to me!"

She glanced back at him, but didn't move toward him. Instead, she reached for the base of the bush.

From behind Alec, answering gunfire exploded.

The other man.

Alec didn't look around. He didn't dare take his eyes off Sergei. Not until Laura was out of there. He wouldn't let that beast touch his wife again.

Laura brought the Mak up fast. Aiming beyond Alec, she pulled the trigger.

Pop, pop, pop.

The sound split the air. She gave with each shot, letting the gun's recoil move her wrists, but not her arms. Bringing the weapon back in place with each tap.

The scream of sirens rose over the gunfire.

Alec waited for any hint of movement, any sign of Sergei at the corner of the house, in the bushes. Laura crouched on the ground, eyes searching behind Alec.

Moments stretched like hours. The sirens grew louder. Closer.

"Laura. Come on."

She started crawling toward him on her hands and knees.

Alec kept his gun leveled on the corner of the house, watching for any hint of Sergei.

Nothing. Sergei and the other thug must have run for it.

Laura crossed the last few feet.

Alec pulled her to his chest. He tried to keep his focus on the bushes, his ears tuned to an approach from behind. But all he could think about was how good she felt in his arms. How warm. How alive. "Are you okay?"

She nodded. Her cheeks were pink from exertion. Scratches from the bushes raised narrow welts on her face and neck.

He wanted to touch her cheeks with his fingertips. He wanted to heal the scratches, to soothe the look of fear from her eyes, to calm the pounding in his own chest. But he couldn't. They didn't have time. "The police are going to be here any second. We have to run for it. Do you think you can do that?"

"They're almost here. We'll never get away." She slumped against him. Wrapping her arms around his shoulders, she held on. "I'm not running anymore, Alec. I can't."

The sirens screamed louder, closer. Winding toward them down the residential street.

Laura was right. They would never get away. They would have to take their chances with the police.

Squad cars swarmed around them. The twilight flashed blue and red in pulsing rhythm, turning the formerly quiet neighborhood into a macabre Fourth-of-July light show.

Alec held her tight. Laura was alive, in his arms. The rest he would figure out. "It's okay, Laura. It's all going to be okay. We're done running."

Chapter Fourteen

Laura set the foam cup on the desk beside her and folded her trembling hands in her lap. She could already feel the caffeine buzzing along her raw nerves. Caffeine was the last thing she or her baby needed. Even two sips. But apparently they didn't offer decaf to detainees. Especially detainees suspected of multiple murders, car theft and kidnapping.

She looked into the wall mirror positioned across the table from her in the plain little box of a room. She didn't have to be the daughter of a cop to know people were watching her from the other side of that one-way reflection. She just wished they'd quit watching and come in to talk to her. The sooner she could explain what was going on, the sooner they could call the FBI.

And the sooner she could see Alec again.

They'd been split up right away. No surprise.

Probably the first thing any local or federal officer learned was the strategy of divide and conquer.

The door to the room opened, and the detective who'd offered her the coffee slipped his head into the room. Dressed in a sharply pressed suit, he was a small, banty rooster of a man. He strutted to the chair closest to her at the table and sat down stiffly, as if his body wouldn't quite bend. "It looks like we have a few things to clear up, Laura."

She took a deep breath. All she had to do was tell the truth. If she told the truth, if she wasn't defensive and didn't try to hide anything, it would all work out. It would all be fine. Isn't that what she'd told Alec? "I'm happy to help clear up whatever questions you have, Detective…"

"Kearney. Your husband has told us quite a story."

Laura frowned. She'd been hoping Alec would come clean with the whole truth, but knowing how paranoid he was about law enforcement, she doubted he had done it this quickly. "I'm glad Alec filled you in. I guess I have nothing to add then."

"Actually, we need to hear the story from you, too."

She gave him her version of events. "I guess that's everything."

"Not quite everything."

She didn't want to have to play games with Detective Kearney. The time for games was long past. "Have you talked to Detective Mylinski?"

"He's in surgery."

"Is he going to be okay?" He had to be okay. Not only did she and Alec need him as an advocate in this mess, but he seemed like a genuinely good cop and a fair man. She couldn't stomach the thought that he might die.

"What does Al Mylinski have to do with this, anyway?"

"We went to him for help."

"Why Mylinski?"

"He's investigating Tony Griggs's death. We thought he could help us. And that we could help him."

The detective seemed to consider this.

Maybe she was getting somewhere. Maybe Kearney was more open to listening to her side of things than she'd originally thought.

"So tell me, Laura, how is Tony Griggs tied up with this?"

"Tony Griggs was killed because of his job as a U.S. marshal. We have evidence. That's why we need to talk to the FBI. Detective Mylinski was going to call Special Agent Callahan for us."

"What kind of evidence do you think you have?"

"Think? We don't think anything. We have evidence. Alec has evidence. He needs to talk to the FBI."

"Listen, you're going to have to talk to me first. If the situation warrants, I'll call the FBI."

"You said you'd talked to Alec."

The detective looked at her blankly.

Just as she'd thought. He'd been playing games. He probably hadn't even seen Alec yet.

She gripped her coffee cup, the foam creaking and bending under the force of her frustration. Maybe she'd been wrong to stay and wait for the police at Detective Mylinski's house. Maybe she should have run, like Alec had wanted to do. Maybe by refusing, she'd destroyed their only chance to reach the FBI, to end this nightmare. "Just contact Special Agent Callahan."

"Who the hell is this Callahan?"

"He specializes in Russian organized crime."

His expressionless face morphed into a look of surprise. "The deaths up in Beaver Falls have something to do with the Russian mob?"

"Yes." She leaned forward in her chair. Maybe now they were getting somewhere. Maybe now he would listen.

"Are you willing to sign a statement that your husband is linked to the Russian mob?"

"Linked? No. He has nothing to do with them."

She shook her head. They were wasting time. "His father is the mobster. His father's men were responsible for what happened in Beaver Falls."

The detective nodded. "How long has your husband been working for his father?"

This was unreal. "My husband had nothing to do with those deaths."

"Listen, Mrs. Martin. The Beaver Falls PD has witnesses that place your husband in that restaurant at the time of the explosion. Are you trying to say he wasn't there?"

"He was there. But he didn't kill those people. And he didn't cause the explosion. He evacuated people in the coffee shop and clothing store next door. He tried to save people."

A rap sounded on the one-way mirror, making Laura jump.

The detective stood, walked to the door and slipped out.

Laura leaned back in her chair. The detective had to at least check out her story, didn't he?

She shook her head. She supposed he didn't have to do anything. Not if he believed she was lying. And that was what he clearly believed. Their only other chance was getting in touch with Bigelow. But if Alec was right, if Bigelow had told Alec's father about their meeting with Mylinski, even that was a dead end.

The door opened. Detective Kearney stepped inside and held the door. A second man entered behind him. Even shorter than Kearney, this man had the shoulders of a bodybuilder. But the way he carried himself and the rich cut of his dark suit suggested something else.

Laura's pulse quickened. The FBI? Had Alec convinced them of the truth? Or had Detective Mylinski recovered enough to make the request?

The detective who had been questioning her stood aside, letting the newcomer slide into the seat next to her. "Mrs. Martin. I have a few questions for you."

She sat forward in her chair and met his gaze. "And I'm happy to answer them, Special Agent."

The man's brows shot up. "'Special Agent'?"

A smile cracked through Kearney's military-straight demeanor.

Laura's hopes plummeted.

"The name is Brearly." He held out his hand. "Detective Brearly. I'm with the Beaver Falls Police Department."

The words hit Laura like a kick to the head. Numbness damped down her alarm, her panic. As if she didn't have enough energy left for panic.

He lowered his hand unshaken. Placing both fists on the table, he leaned toward her, looking down. "I have a few questions. You can answer them now or after I take you and your husband back to Beaver Falls."

"I'm not answering any questions. Not unless I can talk to someone from the FBI."

"These questions aren't about you. We know you weren't at your restaurant when your partner and employees were killed."

"Then why are you asking?" She meant the question as a smokescreen, a way to buy some time, let her think. Because deep down, she knew exactly what Detective Brearly wanted. And she wasn't going to give it to him.

"We are investigating some very serious charges against your husband. We need you to tell us what you know."

"I'm sorry, Detective. You're obviously not interested in listening, so I'm not talking."

"I don't think you understand. We want to know what he told you about those murders. That's all." He dropped his gaze to her belly and then returned it to her face. "Jail is not a nice place. Especially for someone in your condition. You need to think about yourself in all this, Laura. You need to think about your baby."

She met his eyes. She'd been raised to respect the police, and at one time a threat like the one he'd just made would have had her quivering. Not now. After all she'd been through in the past two days, his bluster couldn't come close to fazing her. "I think it's time I talk to a lawyer."

"You don't need a lawyer. Not if you didn't do anything wrong. Just answer my questions."

She shook her head. She wasn't falling for that old line. "I don't have to tell you anything Alec said to me. Not about the restaurant. Not about anything else. He's my husband. Anything he said to me is protected by marital privilege."

THE WALLS WERE CLOSING IN on him.

Alec sat in the tiny room and tried to stay calm. This was his worst nightmare. Stuck in an interrogation room. One cop after another badgering. Treating him like dirt. Like a criminal.

They blended together in his mind, the Madison cop who walked like a military man, the short little bulldog from Beaver Falls, even the female assistant district attorney who'd stopped in to "chat" seemed indistinguishable from the rest. They all asked the same questions, all made the same assumptions. That he was guilty. A murderer. A member of the Russian mob himself.

Laura hadn't told them much. He could tell by the tenor of their questions. And though they'd made general references to her, none of them had said anything specific about her statements. Just as none of them had answered his queries about how she was except with a vague "Fine."

He needed to see her. As the night wore on, she was the only thing he could think about. The only thing he cared about. And if he didn't get to see her soon, make sure she was okay, he was going to strangle the next person to walk through that door.

The door rattled. The knob turned.

Alec braced himself for another cop's scrutiny, another cop's questions, and the inevitable announcement that they were transporting both Laura and him back to Beaver Falls.

The door swung wide and yet another cop strode into the room. His face was gaunt and somber. Shadows cupped sharp cheekbones and settled in the deep sockets of his eyes. And though his body was scarecrow thin, the impeccable dark suit he wore had substance of its own.

"You're FBI, aren't you?"

"Special Agent Callahan."

Alec blew a relieved breath through tight lips. "Did Detective Mylinski call you?"

"Mylinski? No."

If not Mylinski, then who? The cops who'd been trying to railroad him for what happened in Beaver Falls sure hadn't called him. Brearly and the Madison detective, Kearney. Alec had been asking them to for hours, and they'd refused every time. And they'd made it clear as hell they hadn't believed a word he told them. He couldn't picture them changing their minds. "How did you know I was here?"

Callahan folded his long legs into one of the chairs and focused on Alec. "I got a call from Wayne Bigelow. He said you're the son of Ivan Stanislov. And that you might have something I'd be interested in."

Bigelow. Alec clenched his teeth. Had his old buddy found a way to take Ivan's money *and* use Alec and Callahan to write his book? Or maybe Ivan hadn't promised him money, but an interview. Maybe Bigelow was playing all of them like puppets in order to land a big publishing contract. "I wouldn't entirely trust Bigelow."

"Oh?" The word lilted with surprise, but Callahan looked anything but. No doubt he'd pegged Bigelow long ago.

"I think he might be working some kind of deal with my father as well as looking out for me."

"Playing both sides."

"Something like that."

Elbows on table, Callahan tented long fingers and tapped them on his bony chin. "He said Ivan had Tony Griggs killed to get to you."

"That's right."

"How do you know?"

"Griggs was bound with those plastic locking ties. His fingers were broken. Am I right?"

Callahan gave a nod.

"A couple of Sergei Komorov's favorite tricks."

"Maybe. But not conclusive."

"I don't have to be conclusive. I just have to convince you."

"What else?"

"The day after Griggs was killed, Komorov and two other thugs stopped at my wife's restaurant."

"In Beaver Falls."

"One of the women in the restaurant was bound with plastic locking ties and beaten, including having her fingers broken. Just like Tony Griggs." Though Alec was sure Sally had suffered much more. And Traci, too. If there was one thing Sergei was known for, it was his penchant for making his female victims scream.

"The Beaver Falls police are convinced you are the one who's responsible for the deaths and the explosion."

"But you're smart enough not to buy into that garbage."

A shadow of a smile crossed Callahan's face. "And what kind of garbage do you think I should buy?"

Alec sat forward in his chair. He knew what he had to do. The moment he'd promised Laura they'd stop running, he'd known. Now he had to make it work. "You want Ivan Stanislov? I can help you get him."

Callahan said nothing, but judging from the gleam in his eye, the FBI agent was drooling. What FBI agent wouldn't be?

Alec took a sip from the foam cup. The coffee was surprisingly good. He took another sip, biding his time.

Callahan finally opened his mouth. "Okay. I'll bite. How are you going to help me get Ivan Stanislov? I like your ideas about Tony Griggs's murder, but that isn't going to be enough to bring down Stanislov. The state might have a case against Komorov, but I doubt the U.S. attorney could indict anyone with what you've offered. And as they say he could convince a grand jury to indict a ham sandwich."

"I'll meet with my father. Personally. And I'll wear a wire."

Callahan's thin lips quirked upward into a rendition of a smile. "Okay. I can work with that. So what is it you want in return?"

Just the question he was waiting for. "I want this bull about me murdering people and destroying Laura's restaurant to go away."

"Those are very serious charges. The local police say you're a multiple murderer."

"I didn't kill those people. Sergei Komorov did. The locals might not understand that, but you do. Besides, I'm betting I can get my father to confess to those murders. On tape."

Callahan gave a slow nod.

"I want immunity, for myself and for Laura, covering everything that has happened in the past three days."

"Are you saying there are other crimes you might be accused of? Things I haven't heard about yet?" The smile flitted around the edges of his lips and eyes. The look of a cat toying with a mouse before the fatal pounce.

No doubt Callahan had been planning to hold the car theft and kidnapping in reserve, waiting to spring it on Alec when it would do the most good. "I doubt there's anything you haven't heard about."

The smile broke full bore across his lips. "And you think I'll agree to make it all go away?"

"I know you will. If you want my father. And that's not all I want."

"Getting greedy?"

"I want a new identity for Laura and our son."

"And not for yourself?"

Alec nodded. It would be a miracle if he walked

away from what he was about to propose. But if it should work out that way, he supposed he'd need protection. Although without Laura, he wouldn't have much to live for anyway. "For me, too."

"Anything else?"

"Actually, yes. I want to see Laura."

"You'll have plenty of time to see her on the flight to New York."

"Laura's not part of this. I don't want her anywhere near New York."

"Sorry. That I can't give you. Laura's my insurance policy. As long as she's with me, I know you'll hold up your end of the bargain. But don't worry. We'll take good care of her. We'll take good care of you both."

ONE HAND ON THE WHEEL, Sergei slipped open his ringing cell phone and held it to his ear. "Yeah?"

"It's time to come home," Ivan said. "I need you here." The line went dead.

Sergei clipped the phone back on his belt. A cold lump clotted in his gut. If he was brash, he wouldn't go anywhere near New York. He'd stay in Wisconsin. It was nice here. The lakes. The cows. Or maybe he'd go out to Denver. He knew people out there. People he could do business with. He'd sure as hell have more of a future there than he did in New York.

He glared at Pavel tapping away on that damned keyboard in the passenger seat. "Use that computer of yours to book us some plane tickets."

Pavel glanced up, worry written all over that smooth-as-a-baby's-butt face. "Where to?"

He was just a kid, but he knew what letting Nika fall into the cops' hands meant as well as Sergei did. A man didn't fail Ivan Stanislov. Not if he didn't want to pay a price.

But with Ivan Stanislov, a man also couldn't hide. And if they did try to disappear and Ivan caught up with them, the price would be that much dearer.

Sergei looked straight ahead. "New York. Book two tickets to New York. A direct flight."

Chapter Fifteen

Alec pressed against the back of his seat and clutched the armrests, his body shifting to the jiggles and jolts of the taxiing aircraft as it rumbled to the runway. The last time he'd flown was on the plane that had delivered him to Wisconsin, to his life as Alec Martin. Now the plane was taking him back. Back to New York. Back to his father.

And back into the skin of Nikolai Stanislov.

He could feel Laura's gaze from the seat beside him, watching him, reading him. He could smell the sweetness of her scent. He drew a deep breath.

"I never knew you were afraid to fly."

He met her eyes. "I'm not afraid of flying. Landing is something else entirely. At least on this trip."

"Why *are* we flying to New York, Alec? No one has told me anything."

He stopped jiggling his leg. "I made a deal with Callahan."

"I assumed that much. What kind of deal?"

He'd asked Callahan not to say anything to Laura. He wasn't sure how she would react to the prospect of him meeting his father face-to-face, and he wanted more details about how the FBI would handle the risks before he tried to explain. "I'm going to help the FBI bring him down. Just like we planned."

Worry dug a crease between her eyebrows. "How exactly?"

"I'm not sure yet."

"Is it going to be dangerous?"

So much for trying to protect her. She may not know what he'd agreed to with Callahan, but common sense told her it couldn't be easy. "To tell you the truth, I'm not sure what Callahan is thinking. I'm going to talk to him about it when we get to the safe house. I'll tell you everything once I know. I promise."

She nodded, as if she trusted him, but her worry was still there, constricting her lips, lining her forehead.

Pressure descended on his chest like a heavy hand. He searched his mind for something that would make Laura feel better, something that might smooth the worry from her face. "I heard Detective Mylinski made it through surgery."

"Thank God. Do they think he's going to fully recover? No permanent damage?"

"As far as I've heard, it looks good."

A tentative smile curved her lips. It faded almost as soon as it appeared. "What about Wayne Bigelow?"

"I don't know what to think about Bigelow. He called Callahan for us, told him what he knows. Just like he said he would. That's how the FBI got involved in this."

She tilted her head. "So he might *not* have been the one who told your father's men where we were?"

Alec shook his head. "I'd like to think that, but I don't see how it could be. It had to be Bigelow. If not him, I can't explain how Sergei found out." An ache settled heavy in his muscles, in his bones.

"Your friendship with Bigelow meant a lot to you, didn't it?"

"Growing up in that world…" His throat tightened. He didn't know how to explain, how to make Laura understand. He shook his head. "There weren't a lot of people I could trust, that's all. And after I turned my father in, there was nobody."

"Except Bigelow."

He nodded. "And my mother. I could always trust my mother. Of course, I ruined her life."

"That wasn't your doing. That was your father's."

"True. But I had a hand in it all the same." He couldn't think about his mother. Couldn't think about the pain in her eyes the last time he'd seen her. How what he'd done had left her all alone in her final years. He shook his head again, as if he could dislodge those thoughts from his mind. It was impossible.

"And Bigelow?" Laura leaned toward him, her concern genuine, touching.

"When I saw Bigelow again, I really wanted to believe there was someone from my past worth trusting. But as it turned out, the only part of my life as Nika Stanislov worth remembering died with my mother."

"I'm sorry." She slipped her hand over his fist. Sunlight beamed from the window behind her, making her skin glow, turning her hair to gleaming gold.

He savored her scent, soaked in the warmth of her touch. He didn't deserve her. Not her compassion. Not her caring. He wasn't even close. "You're amazing, Laura."

She drew in a breath, holding it as if waiting for him to explain.

"Here you are comforting me, after I betrayed you far more deeply than Bigelow ever betrayed me."

Her lips thinned. For a moment he thought she'd pull her hand away, but she didn't. "I care about you, Alec. But I don't know if I can ever really forgive you. I don't know if I can trust you again."

"I don't expect you to."

Engines rumbled, building to a mind-numbing roar. The plane accelerated, plunging down the runway. Tilting back, it lifted from the earth. Gravity bore down in the center of Alec's chest, as if his heart was struggling to break free, fighting to stay behind in the place he'd once known happiness.

He closed his eyes. As long as Laura was beside him, he could do whatever he needed to do, face whatever he needed to face. He would bring down his father. He would make sure Laura had a life again, a good life for her and their son.

Whether or not he was part of it.

The engines powered on. Shattering gravity's grip, the plane hurtled for New York.

SERGEI PACED the dirty tile floor of the Newark baggage claim and tried to keep his cursing to a low rumble. His feet were tired, his head throbbed and his gut rumbled with hunger. Had he realized the only direct flight between Madison and New York was to Newark, he might have considered a stop in Detroit or some other goddamn place. Now not only did he have to wait for Pavel to try to locate his missing luggage, they would have to sit in a cab for who knew how long to get to Ivan's estate in the Hamptons. The only good thing was they'd been waiting so long at the baggage claim, rush hour had long since passed.

He fingered his phone while glaring at the baggage clerk. He should have called Ivan before they left Madison. Told him they were on their way, maybe asked him to send a car so they didn't have to pay through the nose for a stinking cab. But somehow he couldn't bring himself to do it. Now he was glad he hadn't. He sure as hell didn't want to set foot in one of Ivan's cars without the guns that were in Pavel's bag. He wasn't sure how Ivan would react to them returning without Nika, but he did know he wasn't going to be unarmed when he found out.

Another wave of travelers flooded into the baggage claim and swarmed to one of the carousels like a flock of mindless gulls.

He turned and paced back down the line of conveyor belts. Passing an exit, he stopped dead.

Just outside the glass doors stood Nika and his pregnant wife. And next to them, two men in dark suits that smelled like FBI.

He stepped behind a group of chattering tourists. So it wasn't over. Nika was here in New York. And that meant Sergei still had a chance to reclaim his place in the warm spot.

And take his own revenge.

He smiled despite his aching face. He would taste just how sweet it was. Very soon.

He reached for his phone and flipped it open. He was eager to talk to Ivan now.

Chapter Sixteen

"Nika. How nice to hear from you."

Hatred surged into Alec's throat at the smug sound of his father's voice. He clenched his teeth, his jaw aching. "I want to end this."

"What do you suggest?"

Alec glanced at Special Agent Callahan. They'd been over and over the wheres and hows and whens of the meeting tomorrow. Now all Alec had to do was get his father to agree. "We talk. Face-to-face."

"You're here? In New York?"

"Tomorrow. Twelve o'clock. In a public place." He and Callahan had decided to let his father make the first suggestion of a meeting place. If the location was at all acceptable, they would take it. They wanted him to feel at ease. They wanted him to talk.

"My restaurant in Brighton Beach. Is that public enough for you?"

"Your restaurant in Brighton Beach," Alec repeated as if he was pondering the idea.

Callahan nodded.

"As long as it's open for lunch, that's fine." He wasn't walking into a restaurant populated only by his father and a handful of thugs.

"It will be open. How is my grandson?"

Rage scraped along Alec's nerves until his whole body shook. "We'll talk tomorrow." He punched the off button on Callahan's cell phone and tried to keep from crushing it in his fist.

LAURA STARED out the open window of the modest travel lodge located in a small resort town on the Long Island Sound. Alec had insisted the FBI provide them with separate rooms for her comfort, a kindness she appreciated considering her mixed-up feelings. But it didn't lessen the anxiety rolling in her stomach like water at full boil. It made things worse. If she listened very hard, she could hear the hum of voices through the adjoining door connecting her room with Alec's.

Callahan and Alec discussing their plan.

She took a deep breath. The salt air carried a hint of cigarette smoke, evidence that the agent positioned outside her door was still there, though she couldn't see him from the window. All she could see was the masked chain-link fence of the amusement park next door. A large clown face loomed above the fence. A giant tongue lolling from its open mouth formed a slide. She could imagine that when bathed in the summer sun and giggles of families who flocked to the Long Island Sound from the city, the clown slide would seem cute, harmless. But in the evening gloom of late April's rain and fog and chill, it was pure taunting menace.

Or maybe her reaction was due to the feeling of impending doom gripping the back of her neck.

Turning away from the window, she paced the floor. She hated feeling so out of control. So helpless. She needed to know what was going on in Alec's room, what he and Callahan were planning. The idea of sitting in this room staring at the blank white walls—or worse yet, that horrendous clown slide—while they determined something so important made her physically ill.

She paused next to the door that lead to Alec's room. Situated at the corner of the building, his window looked out onto the back parking lot and the FBI surveillance van. A reminder of why they were here. What they were facing. And the secrecy she couldn't penetrate.

Maybe she would rather have a view of the clown slide.

A sound reached her from the other room. The thunk of a door closing. Followed by silence.

She held her breath. No shuffle of movement. No muffled voices hashing out plans. Had Callahan left? Was Alec alone?

She stepped closer to the adjoining door. On the flight, Alec had promised to tell her everything once he and Callahan had determined the plan. And she aimed to hold him to it. With a trembling hand, she unlocked her side and pulled it open. Balling her hand into a fist, she tapped the remaining barrier with her knuckles.

A lock scraped free. Alec pulled open the door. Circles dug deep under tired gray eyes. Creases of tension and concern flanked his mouth. Dark stubble shadowed cheeks and chin.

Her heart shifted in her chest. He looked as if he'd been through hell. "What's the plan?"

He swung the door wide. "Come in."

"I have to know, Alec."

"I know."

Stepping into the room, she glanced around. She half expected Callahan to be skulking in the corner, ready to silence any information Alec might tell her. To her relief, the room was empty.

"I talked to my father."

"Oh my God." She stepped toward him, wanting to reach out, wanting to touch him. No wonder he looked as if he'd been through hell. He had. "What happened? What did he say?"

"I'm meeting with him tomorrow. At one of his restaurants. I'm wearing a wire."

Alarm ripped her self control. She grabbed his arm. "No. You can't."

"It's the only way to make sure—"

"He'll kill you."

"Callahan has a plan. The FBI will be just outside. They'll be listening the whole time. They'll get me out safely."

"Plans can go wrong. Things you can't foresee can change everything. It's too dangerous. You can't go through with it, Alec."

"I have to."

"No, you don't. The FBI can find evidence against him other ways. Forensics. Wire taps. They don't need you to risk your life."

His lips thinned to a bloodless line. The muscle along his jaw clenched and unclenched, but he didn't answer.

He couldn't really expect to stroll into his father's restaurant, have a chat with the monster and stroll back out again. The plan was crazy. Suicide. Why would he agree to something like that? "On the plane you said you made a deal. What did he give you in exchange?"

"Immunity for everything that happened the past few days."

"For the explosion at the Blue Ox?"

He nodded.

"You don't need immunity for that. You didn't do anything wrong."

"The cops have evidence that says I did."

"Evidence that won't stand up to a strong wind." She let her hand slide down his arm and caught his fingers in hers. She had to make him see that he didn't have to do this. She had to make him listen to her. To reason. "They can't pin what happened at the Blue Ox on you on the word of some people you evacuated. All those people can testify to is that you saved their lives."

"Unless the Makarov pistol the cops took from us is the weapon that shot Traci and the produce delivery man."

The pieces shifted together in Laura's mind. The weapon had been taken by the cops at Detective Mylinski's house. By now it was probably logged in at the ballistics lab, awaiting testing. "You're afraid the slugs will match."

He nodded.

"So we tell them where we got the gun. And more evidence will turn up. If we hire a lawyer, if we tell the truth, I don't see how they could convict you of anything. You don't need to make some suicidal deal with Callahan."

He looked down at her. Shadows settled around his eyes, making them appear dark, hollow. "I didn't make the deal for the immunity, Laura. Not totally."

She searched his eyes. "Your father."

He didn't need to nod.

"This isn't the only way to put him on death row, Alec."

"Maybe not, but it's the surest. And the easiest."

"For who? The FBI?"

"I need this, too. For my own piece of mind. I need to look into his eyes. I need to bring him down."

"Why? For revenge?"

"It's not that simple."

She blew out a frustrated breath. "None of this is simple. None of this is easy. And it won't be for a long time. But that doesn't mean you need to sacrifice yourself."

"I'm not sacrificing myself. I'm working with Callahan and the FBI to make sure I walk out of that restaurant alive."

"Callahan can't ensure your safety. No matter what he says."

"We've talked about the risks. We've planned for them."

"You can't plan for things you can't foresee. I should know. I planned each detail of my life. But the past few days changed everything."

He looked away from her, but not before she saw the hurt in his eyes. The regret.

"I'm sorry. I didn't mean that as an attack."

"The FBI have done this kind of thing before. Callahan knows what he's doing."

She shook her head. She had to reach him. She had to make him understand. "He may be the very best, that has nothing to do with it. There are things you can't control. Things no one can control."

Like loving Alec. Like, despite everything that had happened, *still* loving him.

Chills rippled through her. Weakness pooled in her knees.

"I have to do this, Laura. Please try to understand that."

She searched for more words, words that would convince him, words that would make him understand. Her tongue lodged thick in her mouth. Emotions tangled and swirled inside her. Emotions she'd done her best to deny, to control. Emotions more powerful than she was. "I don't want to lose you."

His eyebrows dipped low. His eyes cut through her like gray lasers.

"I know I said I wasn't sure I could forgive you. That I didn't know if I could trust you again. And I still don't know. But maybe those things just don't happen right away. Maybe forgiveness and trust take time. I'm willing to give it time, Alec. I'm willing to give *us* time. But I can't do that if you get yourself killed."

"Oh, Laura. I love you. More than I thought I could love anyone." He gathered her into his arms. Reaching a hand to her cheek, he brushed away tears.

She hadn't even known she was crying. But suddenly it was all she could do. Cry for Alec. For herself. For their baby. Tears ripped from her heart, her soul. She couldn't control them. She couldn't control anything anymore.

And she didn't try.

ALEC CLOSED HIS EYES and leaned his cheek against Laura's hair.

Sob after sob trembled though her body. The strain, the fear, the horrors of the last few days washed from her in waves.

What he wouldn't give to be able to let loose like that. To cleanse the horrors from his eyes. Rinse away the fear weighing on his mind. Flush the dread festering in his gut. As it was, he could only hold her. Stroke her hair. Wipe her tears. Let her dispel the tension for both of them.

God, he loved her.

Hope surged in his chest, welling like pride. She was willing to give them another chance. It was all he could ask for. The answer to his prayers. The realization of his dreams.

He would figure out a way to make it work. He would make sure he walked away from the meeting tomorrow. He would grab hold of this second chance with both hands. "I'll take care of everything, Laura. We'll have a future. I promise."

She looked up at him, her eyes red, her cheeks streaked with tears. She opened her mouth, then closed it again without speaking. As if she too recognized they had just stepped beyond words.

He lowered his head and fitted his lips to hers.

She tasted of salt and sweet, tears and happy times. She wove her arms around his neck and twined her fingers in his hair. Her belly pressed against him, soft yet firm.

He absorbed her scent, her taste, the warmth of her arms around him, locking it away in his memory, in his heart, in his soul. She made him a better man. Just by the way she looked at him, the way she touched him. Just by being near. As if her touch, her kiss, the look in her eyes gathered the scattered pieces of him and brought him together.

He needed that tonight, more than ever before. He needed her. "I want to make love to you."

He braced himself, waiting for her to pull away, but she didn't. Instead, she eased her hands down his back and grasped the hem of his shirt. Slowly she skimmed it up his body and over his head.

Cool air kissed his skin, followed by the heat of her touch, her gaze.

He unbuttoned her maternity top, his fingers fumbling. He needed to touch her, to feel her, to claim her. He slid the blouse off her shoulders. He unclasped her bra and slipped it down her arms.

Her body had changed with pregnancy, grown lush and voluptuous. Her breasts hung round and full and heavy. Dusky nipples puckered, dark against her almost translucent skin.

"You are so beautiful." Gathering her warmth and softness against him, he kissed her. He opened his mouth, plunging deep, joining his tongue with hers.

Her hands glided over his back, his shoulders. Rubbing his skin, stoking his need.

He lowered his lips, riffling kisses along her jaw, down her neck over her collarbone. He captured a nipple, drawing it into his mouth, teasing it with his tongue. He could spend his whole life touching her, tasting her, and it wouldn't be enough. He'd never get enough.

Nipping and suckling one breast and then the other, he pushed her maternity pants and panties down her legs and smoothed his hands over her belly. He couldn't believe how beautiful she was. How full with the life they'd created. "Such a miracle. You are such a miracle."

She combed her fingers through his hair, sending chills down his spine and fanning out over his skin.

He lowered himself to his knees and littered kisses over the firm roundness of her belly, soaking in her scent, nibbling her skin. Moving lower, he followed the stripe of smooth skin darkened by pregnancy that led from her navel to the hair between her legs.

He wanted to taste her, be part of her, experience everything about her. He skimmed his hands up her sides and eased her down to a sitting position on the edge of the bed. Then he kissed lower, coaxing her to lean back, to open her thighs, until he could savor her.

He teased her with his tongue, dancing over the most sensitive part of her and then dipping deep. She was impossibly sweet, as if pregnancy had ripened her, making her tender and delicious as mellow fruit. He gripped her open legs, pulling her close, devouring her.

A moan rose to her lips. And then a whimper.

One shudder then another seized her body, sending her muscles into spasm.

When her body finally relaxed, he worked his way back to her lips. He cuddled her close, kissing her lips, her neck, her breasts.

She laid a hand on his chest, pushing him into a standing position.

Night air cooled where her body had warmed. For a moment he thought she was pushing him away, that she'd changed her mind, her heart. But then her hands moved up his thighs. She unbuttoned his jeans and lowered the zipper. Hooking her fingers under his waistband, she pushed both jeans and briefs down his legs.

He sprang free, hard and urgent.

She circled his tip with her tongue before taking him into her mouth. Warmth and wetness surrounded him. She moved her lips up and down his length, sucking him, driving him to ecstasy, driving him mad.

Finally he gripped her shoulders, stilling her movement. "I want this to last. I want to be inside you."

"I want you inside me, too." Her voice was rough, husky with a need of her own.

His heart lurched against his ribcage. Heat pulsed in his groin.

She turned on the bed and crawled to its center on hands and knees. Her belly swung like a cradle beneath her, full and round and ripe. Stopping, she looked at him over her shoulder, waiting for him. Her glistening lips curved into a smile.

Electricity crackled through his blood. Every nerve in his body demanded he claim her, join with her, be one with her. He'd never needed anything as much as he needed her now.

He followed her onto the bed. Rising on his knees behind her, he positioned himself at her gate. Slowly, gently, he pushed into her.

She was so soft. So warm. Her body took him in. Accepted him. Embraced him. A whisper rose from her lips. Wordless, but aching with need. Need for him.

And an answering need reached his own lips. It built with each push into her softness. It quickened with each breath. He slid his hands over the silk of her back, tracing the length of her backbone. Reaching her shoulders, he skimmed down her arms and then up.

Her breasts swayed in rhythm to his strokes. He molded his hands over their full curves, kneading her softness, pinching the stiff peaks of her nipples until a moan of pleasure vibrated through her chest.

He wanted to know all of her, absorb all of her.

He moved one hand down, caressing the weight of her belly, savoring the feel of firm life inside her. More precious than his own breath. He stroked the curl of hair between her legs with his fingers. Burrowing lower, he found the most tender part of her.

"Alec," she gasped, the word almost a plea.

He slid his fingers between her silken folds with each thrust he made. Faster. Harder. He wanted this to be good for her. He wanted it to be great.

Her breathing came fast, rough. She threw her head back. Blond hair cascaded over her back. Rocking against him, she took him deeper, swallowed him whole.

He kept moving, his body, his fingers. He couldn't stop if he tried. He'd rather die than stop now.

Her body gripped him. Muscles pulsing and squeezing. Pulling him toward the edge. Oh, so close to the edge.

He gritted his teeth. He couldn't let go. Not now. Not yet. "Laura, look at me. I have to see your eyes."

She rolled to her side without breaking rhythm, without pulling away. Brushing hair from her face with one hand, she met his gaze.

Love seized and pulsed through him on a wave

of fire, turning his muscles to water, shaking him with physical force. And for a moment he was that man in her eyes. The man she inspired him to be.

He let go, joining her in bliss, crying out her name.

Chapter Seventeen

The low scream of a siren grated in Alec's ear like a mosquito's whine. He forced open an eye and tried to gain his bearings. The hotel room was dim, still deep in night's shadow. Laura's hair tickled his cheek. Lying on her side, she snuggled her back to his chest. Her soft, naked warmth pushed against his lap.

Need stirred in his blood. The air smelled of salt and sex and her warm sweetness. He closed his eyes again. He wanted the night to stretch endlessly. He wanted to stay in this dream forever.

The siren grew louder. Closer.

No use.

Careful not to wake Laura, he untangled his limbs from hers. He twisted in the direction of the siren—the open door that led to Laura's adjoining room. Light pulsed red through the door frame.

Adrenaline slammed into his blood. He sat up,

his pulse tripping. Peeling back the covers, he slipped from the bed.

Laura didn't stir. The stress of the past few days, the fear, the lack of sleep, had finally taken its toll. Just as well. If she had reason to get up, he'd wake her. If the sirens, the lights amounted to nothing, it was better she slept.

He pulled the blankets around her. But even as he did, he knew his hope the lights meant nothing was an empty husk. Goose bumps rose on his bare skin, but the chills weren't due to temperature. Something had happened. Something bad. He could feel it with each pulse of red light.

He found his jeans on the floor and pulled them on. Pausing, he glanced back at Laura, but something wouldn't let him wake her. She'd been through so much. He didn't want to put her through one more thing. Not unless he had to.

He slipped through the door and into Laura's vacant room. He curled his fingers into a fist and then straightened them, opening and closing. What he wouldn't give to have one of those cursed Makarovs in his hand about now. FBI guard or no, Alec felt exposed, vulnerable.

He approached the window from the side so no one outside would see his shadow. No matter what was happening, he didn't want his presence known. Sidling close to the pane, he eased the sheers aside with a finger.

Red and blue swirled and pulsed in the fog rolling in off the sound, making the air throb like a living thing. Judging from the lights, police cars huddled beyond the masked chain-link fence of the amusement park next door. The white slats woven through the fence blocked his view of the cars and cops, but above the barrier, a clown face peered at him from the top of a giant slide.

A spotlight flashed between the slats. Light glared right at him, then bounded away.

Alec stepped to the side, letting the curtain fall. What were they looking for? Him? he didn't think so. The light's erratic movement suggested they were trying to point the spotlight's beam, trying to see something less easy to focus on than a hotel room.

Darkness safely shrouding the window once again, Alec teased back the sheers and peered outside.

The spotlight beamed into the fog. Sure and steady, it caught the clown's face. Curves of white cheeks and garish lips grinned stark in the glare. The giant red tongue that formed the slide glistened, as if heavy humidity had condensed, giving it the moisture of a living tongue.

No. Not condensation.

Alec stared at the clown's open mouth. A body lay at the tongue's crest. Head hanging down, blood drained from a slashed throat and coursed down the lolling tongue. A shock of white hair caught the light.

Wayne Bigelow.

Grief and anger worked up Alec's throat like bile. Damn, damn, damn. His father had done this. He had no doubt. Once Bigelow had directed Komorov to the detective's house, Ivan had needed the reporter for only one last thing. To send a message.

A message Alec received loud and clear.

Fear knifed into his stomach and twisted, catching and grating like a rusty blade. His father knew where they were. And FBI protection or no, he could reach them at any time.

Alec let the curtain fall. Racing back into the room where Laura was sleeping, he gathered his shirt and shoes from the floor and pulled them on. He glanced one last time at Laura's sleeping form. A weight descended into his chest, sinking lower with each painful throb of his heart.

He'd tried so hard. So hard to protect her. So hard to be the man she deserved, the man he wanted so much to be. And now he had a second chance. *They* had a second chance. A chance for happiness. A chance for family.

A chance his father had just taken away.

He couldn't be the husband Laura deserved, the father his son deserved, the man he ached to be. Not if he wanted to protect Laura and their baby. He hadn't wanted to see it. He'd tried to pretend the law could protect them, that the courts could dole out justice for them. He couldn't deny the truth any longer.

He would never be rid of his father's legacy of crime and violence. Not until he and Laura were both dead and their son was in Ivan Stanislov's hands. And not only would Alec die before he let that happen—he would kill.

In cold blood.

SERGEI LEANED BACK in the recliner and drew in the rich scent of Italian leather. It was good to be back in New York. Good to be back in Ivan's home on the ocean, savoring the good life. The life he'd earned.

He lifted one of Ivan's glasses, filled to the rim with the best imported vodka on the rocks, just the way he liked it. Ice cubes chimed against crystal. The sound of celebration.

The reporter had died well. Quiet and bloody. And his body had been light, easy to carry to the top of the slide. He wished he could see Nika's face when he awakened in the morning to the sight of his friend's body. He would pay to see the horror in his eyes.

He took a long sip from his glass. He would see Nika soon enough. Tomorrow Nika would be theirs.

And the woman would be his.

His groin tightened and the thought of what he'd do to her. How he would bruise her pretty face. How he would snap her elegant fingers one by one. How her screams would ring like sweet music in his ears.

He'd stepped so close to failure this time. If it hadn't been for Nika's trip to New York, if it hadn't been for a chance meeting at the airport, he would be lying low in a dirty apartment in the Bronx, not here drinking to the crash of ocean waves. Not back in the warm spot where he belonged.

"It is done?"

Sergei turned at the low voice and peered into the hall.

Ivan strode out of the shadows, a red silk robe draped his shoulders. A gold belt girded his middle. The study's dim light fell on a face as smooth as Pavel's and made the silver in his dark hair and mustache sparkle. Built strong like a bull, he moved with a czar's imperial manner. Every step he took commanded respect. Every order he issued demanded fear.

But Sergei was afraid of no man. He took a long drink from his glass before he answered. "Nika and the FBI will be waking to an interesting sight. A show of our power."

The corners of Ivan's thin lips quirked.

Whether it was a smile, a snarl or a trick of shadow, Sergei couldn't tell. "When can I take the woman?"

"You are impatient?"

Sergei spent his life being impatient. "I want my revenge."

"Ah, revenge is the sweetest form of passion."

Sergei recognized the old Russian proverb. "I have waited as long as you."

"You will wait longer. I want my grandson healthy. I will not take him from his mother until it is his time."

Sergei ground his teeth, crushing an ice cube between molars. That couldn't be long. The woman looked as if she would burst any moment. But he didn't want to wait. "The child can be cut from his mother's belly. It will make him tough."

Ivan walked behind Sergei's chair, the tap of his slippers on the parquet floor slow and regular as a dripping faucet. "You nearly failed me this time."

Sergei swallowed. Ice shards slipped cold down his throat. "I brought him back to you."

"The FBI brought him back."

"He's here. That is all that's important. I told you where they were hiding him."

"There would have been no need for the FBI to get involved. Not if you had handled things the way we agreed."

Anger hardened in Sergei's gut. "We have faced them before. Has prison softened you, Ivan? Are you now afraid of the FBI?"

A crash sounded from the bar behind Sergei's chair, a glass shattering on the hard floor.

"Pavel." Ivan barked into the intercom next to the bar. "Get in here. I have a mess for you to clean up."

Sergei couldn't help but smile. Maybe Ivan's days were fading. Maybe he was getting older at heart than he looked in face. Maybe it was Sergei's time to not only bask in the sun's rays, but to become the sun itself.

"I am not afraid of anyone, Sergei." Ivan's voice was quiet, but close behind. "But if you were smart, you would be."

Sergei tried to twist around in the recliner, to see Ivan's eyes. But the knife drew across his throat before he could move.

"No one fails Ivan Stanislov."

Sergei's life gushed hot down his chest. And the world went black.

Chapter Eighteen

Alec stepped out into the humid salt air and closed the hotel's door quietly behind him. Fog clung to his skin like clammy sweat. His pulse throbbed in his ear, ticking off the time. He had to find a way out of here and to his father's house. Soon dawn would come, and his chance would be gone. He didn't have a minute to waste.

The hotel was surrounded. Cops on one side, FBI on the other. He had to find a way out with neither spotting him.

"What are you doing out here?"

Alec's heart seized, then resumed beating. He turned in the direction of the voice.

Ash glowed from the end of the FBI agent's cigarette. He stood with his back to the hotel's brick wall. His face flashed red and blue in the police lights.

"I wanted to see the show." He gestured to the

clown slide. "Where were you when this happened?"

"Right here. I was the first to notice the body."

"And you didn't notice how it got there?"

He shrugged, as if that part didn't matter.

The hell it didn't. "One of Ivan Stanislov's men is responsible. That man is Wayne Bigelow. He works for the *Brooklyn Chronicle*. His death is a message for me."

The man cocked his head. "You think?"

Alec let the sarcasm roll off his back. It was no surprise the guy felt defensive. He'd screwed up. Big-time. But Alec was most concerned about what would happen from here on out. "Why are local cops here? Where are the FBI?"

"Callahan's on top of it." He sucked a drag off the cigarette, the ash flaring red.

"Where is Callahan?"

"On the other side of the fence. You want to see him? He said he'd be back in about five minutes."

Five minutes. Just enough time for Alec to slip away, yet not so much time that Laura would be in danger. Especially with the number of cops next door. As Laura was fond of reminding him, not *all* of them could be crooked.

Besides, if Sergei, or whoever had killed Bigelow, had wanted to reach Laura and him tonight, he would have done it before drawing so much police attention.

The only thing Alec had to do was figure out how he could slip away unnoticed. "I can't wait five minutes. I have to talk to Callahan now."

The guy groaned.

"Go over to the fence and shout to him," Alec said.

"I'm not leaving you alone out here."

"I'll go back inside."

The special agent didn't look convinced.

"I need to talk to him now. It's about my father. He's going to want to hear what I have to say."

The man nodded to the hotel door. "Go back in the room."

Alec turned, but before he returned to the room, he glanced back over his shoulder. "Thanks." He opened the door and stepped inside.

The special agent started across the small parking area and approached the fence.

Alec slipped back out the door, closing it behind him. He raced down the sidewalk outside the rooms and slipped into a utility hall. Jammed with vending and ice machines, the hall stretched through the middle of the travel lodge. He dashed through the dark hallway. Emerging on the other side, he slowed to a walk. He had to get out of here as quickly as he could but couldn't afford to attract attention.

Streetlights glowed from the road, their illumination fuzzy in the fog. The travel lodge sat on a sweeping turn lined with trees. On the other side of the road, the fog hovered too thick to see through. But Alec didn't need to see. The gritty salt air and light crash of waves told him all he needed to know.

He hurried across the parking lot toward the bend in the road. If he could cross the street before the turn, trees would hide him from police clustered at the amusement park gate. Then he could make for the water, relying on the slope of the beach, retaining walls and playgrounds to shield him as he ran in the direction of town.

Headlights swung into the motel's driveway.

Alec dashed the last few yards. He plunged into the grove of trees and bushes. He squatted down, praying the vegetation, the fog and the darkness would hide him.

The headlight beams shifted, moving over Alec's hiding place like glowing apparitions. The car moved past.

Alec let out a breath of relief. Climbing to his feet, he wove through underbrush until he reached the road. He ran across, then took an angle through the parking lot and down to the beach.

Sand shifted under his shoes. The moist air made his lungs ache. He had to hurry. He had to get out of town and on his way to his father's house before the FBI knew he was gone. Before they came looking for him.

He reached the water's edge. Waves broke and crashed to the shore, masking the rasp of his breathing, the beat of his heart. The sand was firmer here, easier to run across. He launched into a good pace, his shoes crunching on seashells with each step.

To his right, the police lights pulsed in the night, the fog swirling red and blue. He pushed his legs to move faster. The beach narrowed, reaching its end. He followed its line as far as he could, then angled back toward the road.

Well past the amusement park, he ran along the boardwalk skirting the shore. His shoes scraped sand scattered over the wood planks. Moving toward the center of town, boardwalk gave way to the sidewalk.

Lungs screaming for more oxygen, he slowed to a jog. He glanced into each driveway he passed. He needed a car. Without tools, cracking the steering column so he could start the vehicle would be tough. But he had to figure out a way. He still had miles to go before he reached his father's house on Long Island's eastern tip.

He passed empty driveway after empty driveway, all cars safely locked behind garage doors. He kept running. Waiting for a siren on his tail. Dawn was closing in fast. He probably only had a couple of hours of darkness left. Not to mention the FBI would be on his heels any minute. He had no time to lose.

The houses gave way to a smattering of cafés and boat repair shops. A sign loomed out of the fog. Its reflective surface pointed the way to a marina.

A marina. Perfect. He followed the sign. A boat would be faster than any car, the route more direct, and the approach more unexpected. Just what he needed.

He ran up the crest of a hill, away from the surf. On the way down the slope on the other side, a bay opened before him.

Ghostly outlines of piers lined the dull blackness of water. Fingers jutted from each long pier, forming slips between. Boats ranging from small sailboats to medium-size yachts filled each slip, bobbing on the water.

Alec scrutinized the vessels. He picked out an uncovered day cruiser docked at the end of one of the long stretches of pier. It had an open console and was small enough that it probably wouldn't have an elaborate security system, yet large enough to give him the speed he needed.

He raced down the hill to the marina. He knew little about boats. He'd ridden on his father's yacht as a kid, but his father had never allowed him to drive. He could only hope the ignition was similar enough to a car's that he could figure out how to start the engine.

Passing what looked like a clubhouse building, he bounded onto the long pier and ran for the boat he'd picked out.

"Hey! What are you doing out there?"

Oh, hell.

He veered off onto the finger dock. Blood pulsed in his ears. Just his luck this marina employed a security guard. And that the guard happened to be awake, even at this hour.

Alec leaped onto the boat. He clawed at the line securing the boat at the stern. Unwinding it from the cleat, he tossed it into the water. Another line secured the front of the boat. He had to untie it and get the hell out of here before the security guard reached him. He scrambled over seats. One shoe hit a discarded beer bottle. It rolled and skidded. He grabbed the side of the console, regaining his balance. Scrambling across seats and around the console, he reached the cleat at the bow.

Footsteps thundered toward him on the pier.

Pulse racing, he freed the front of the boat and

scrambled behind the wheel. Pushing the button on the throttle that lowered the engine into the water, he checked the ignition with a hand.

No key.

He had no tools. No way to crack the steering column. No way to turn the ignition once he did.

The footsteps came closer. The guard had almost reached the finger docks surrounding the slip.

Pulse thrumming, Alec ran his hands along the sides of the console. There had to be tools onboard somewhere. He needed to find them. Now. He thrust his fingers under the edge of seat cushion. His fingertips hit something metal.

The ignition key.

He grabbed it, jammed it into the ignition and turned. The engine leaped to life. He pulled the throttle lever in reverse. The boat chugged backward, out of the slip.

A shadow loomed just as the boat cleared the finger dock. Did the guard have a gun?

Alec didn't wait to find out. He jammed the throttle forward. The engine churned. Moist wind buffeted his face. The boat gained speed.

He wove around buoys, sliced through the no-wake zone with treacherous speed. Pushing the boat to its limit, he shot under the bridge and out into the sound.

THE SHEETS NEXT TO LAURA were cool when she awoke. She blinked in the darkness, trying to discern Alec's outline.

Where had he gone?

She sat up in bed. Sheets fell to her waist, exposing swollen breasts, nipples tender from Alec's mouth. The skin of her cheeks and breasts and thighs burned hot, scraped by the stubble on Alec's chin. Even the very core of her was sore, deliciously sore, and the ache made her feel warm inside. Loved. "Alec?"

No answer.

She moved slowly, heaving her body up from the bed. The room was still, quiet, no hiss of a shower. No rustle of movement from the next room. No noise of any kind. Foreboding pulsed along her nerves.

She didn't want to turn on the light. Didn't want anyone outside to know she was awake. Not until she found Alec. Not until she made certain everything was okay.

She picked up her clothes from the floor. Her panties and bra. Her pants and maternity blouse. One by one she pulled them on in the dark with shaking hands. She didn't find one piece of Alec's clothing, though they had left them mixed on the floor. She groped the floor for socks and shoes.

Once dressed, she padded to the door that

joined the two rooms. Her fingers brushed the cold steel barrier. A shiver peppered her skin. She didn't remember closing the door.

She was sure she hadn't.

Had Alec closed it? Was he afraid of waking her? Was she letting her fear get the best of her for no reason?

She took hold of the knob, twisted and pulled the door open a crack. She peered through the small space. The room glowed and throbbed with an eerie light. Faint voices niggled at her ear.

She'd left the window open, the stretch of glass shrouded by sheers alone. But what were the voices? What was the light?

She opened the door a little wider and took a cautious step into the room. This room seemed empty, too. The bathroom door hung open, no one inside.

Where had Alec gone?

She slipped into the room and walked to the window. Moving the sheers aside with a trembling hand, she peered into the night.

The amusement park pulsed with a mixture of flashing police lights and the glare of spotlights. Over the fence, the clown slide emerged from thick fog. Harsh light and deep shadow turned the grinning face into a garish image straight from a horror film. Two men hovered at the top of the slide. Backs to her, they seemed to be studying something she couldn't see. A camera's flash ignited the fog like an explosion of fireworks.

Fear seized her, shaking so hard she could hardly stand.

A knock sounded on her door.

Laura jumped. She yanked her hand from the sheers, letting them drape back over the window. "Alec?" She held her breath, waiting, hoping, praying it was him.

"Laura? It's Callahan."

She exhaled with a whoosh. Maybe Callahan knew where Alec was. He had to know. Nothing could have happened to Alec. There had to be another explanation for the police outside.

Moving to the door, she checked through the peephole before opening the door.

Callahan stepped inside without waiting for an invitation. "Where's Alec?"

"I don't know." Her voice eeked from a tight throat, high, shrill. If she hadn't felt the vibration in her own vocal chords, she wouldn't have recognized it as her own.

Callahan glanced around the room, as if expecting Alec to be hiding in the shadows. Completing his visual sweep, he focused again on her. "When was the last time you saw him?"

"What's happening out there? Why are the police here?"

"When was the last time you saw your husband?" he repeated, enunciating each word as if talking to a hysterical child.

"I fell asleep. I don't know what time. When I woke up, he wasn't here. Where is he?"

Callahan's eyebrows dropped low over his sunken eyes. "I think your husband has given us the slip."

"What?" She couldn't have heard him right. The baby gave a good kick, making her gasp. As if he had felt the dose of adrenaline surging through her bloodstream.

Laura shook her head. None of this made sense. Why would Alec sneak away from the men protecting them? Why would he leave *her?*

She looked out the open door, at the lights, at the clown. Sweat broke out on the back of her neck. "What is going on out there?"

Shadows cupped Callahan's cheekbones and pooled in his eyes. "A body was found in the amusement park."

"A body?" Not Alec's. He wouldn't have asked where Alec was if the body was Alec's. She forced herself to breathe. In and out. In and out. "Whose body?"

"Wayne Bigelow."

"Bigelow?" Her head whirled. She couldn't think. She couldn't wrap her mind around what he was telling her. "Wayne Bigelow was killed? In the amusement park? How?"

Callahan didn't answer. He merely stared at her, the shadows and his expression of worry distorting his face, making it look even more like a skull.

"Why?"

"Because Ivan Stanislov wanted him dead. He wanted to send a message."

"He knows we're here." Pieces shifted in her mind. A shudder claimed her. "He didn't take Alec. Please, he couldn't have taken Alec."

"No. I'm afraid your husband left here of his own free will."

Suddenly she knew where Alec had gone. She knew what he was about to do. What he felt he *had* to do. What he might already have done. Despair penetrated her chest and punctured her heart. Helplessness. "He can't do it. He's a good man. He can't do it."

"Do what, Laura?"

"Kill his father."

Chapter Nineteen

Alec hadn't seen his father's house for more than thirteen years, but he had no trouble picking it out from the other mansions lining the shore. The Tudor-style roof rose and peaked in layers, thrusting into the sky. Gray stone shifted in and out of the fog. Huge expanses of mullioned glass stared out on the sea, black as soulless eyes.

Acid churned in the pit of his gut. He'd tried so hard to escape this place and all it meant. The brutality, the depravity, the violence. The legacy he had never wanted. And yet now he was back. About to commit a cold-blooded act that would cement his place in that legacy. Murder. "Welcome home, Nika," he muttered. "Welcome home."

He set his chin. At least his son would never be a part of this world. He had to grab on to that, use it to carry him through the next hours.

Through the rest of his life. Better for his son to not know him than for him to allow his child to be sucked into this life. This nightmare.

He piloted the boat around a curve in the coast and into a small bay. The private marina where his father had kept his yacht and sailboats still lined one quiet shore. A single small sailboat bobbed on the wake as Alec slowed and glided into an empty slip. The day cruiser's hull scraped along wood and rubber, finally jolting to a stop.

Reaching to the seat next to him, he picked up the razor knife and flat-headed screwdriver he'd found flanking the boat's console. The knife's blade was sharp, its handle cold and slick in his palm. He'd rather have a gun. But he didn't have that choice. He had to take what he could get.

He jumped to the pier and left the boat drifting free in the slip. He scanned the fog, trying to spot any sign of movement stirring against the hulking shapes of trees. He saw nothing, heard nothing above the lapping waves. Satisfied he was alone, he started in the direction of the house.

Even under fog, it didn't take him long to negotiate the familiar paths and skirt the coastline he'd explored as a child. Soon he was standing outside the fence surrounding his father's estate.

He eyed the wrought iron stretching high above him. The points on the top pierced into the fog. To a stranger contemplating scaling this fence, it might seem daunting. To him it was nothing. He'd conquered it before he'd turned ten years old.

Stuffing the screwdriver in his pocket and clenching the knife between this teeth, he grasped the fence, the iron cold and slick under his hands. Bracing his feet on the side of the stone pillar, he supported his weight. Hand over hand, he pulled himself up the plain iron bars. When he reached the top, he inched along the scroll work until he could grasp the stone pillar. He climbed on top of its concrete cap, avoiding the iron spikes.

From his vantage point, hidden by fog and trees, he had a clear view of the house. The swimming pool curved along the far end of the house, surrounded by elaborate lighted landscaping and cloaked by a custom cover. Next to it stretched manicured lawns and gardens bursting with tulips and flowering bushes. Closest to the corner where he clung, the yards deepened into a private tangle of trees and big-leafed hosta lilies.

The windows on this side of the house were dark. Nothing but a few yard lights diffused by the fog. This was his father's private wing. His sitting room. His elaborate bathroom. His bedroom.

This is where Alec would slip inside.

He eyed the French doors. Each had wood panels on the bottom and mullioned glass above, echoing the style of the countless windows. And each was wired with an alarm. He had to find a way inside without opening doors or windows.

He lowered himself down the inside of the fence. A few feet from the ground, he jumped. The force of his fall jarred up his legs, but he didn't have time to notice. At any moment someone could emerge from the lighted part of the house. At any time he could be spotted.

Crouching low, he gripped the knife in his hand and raced into the shade garden. He stole along the edge of trees, betting on the fog for cover. As long as his father hadn't developed a sudden liking for dogs in recent years, Alec should make it.

He reached the house. No dogs. No thugs. He crept to the French door closest to the trees and knelt at its base.

He fitted his fingers against the wood panels at the base of the glass. He inserted the razor knife at the ridge between panel and molding and sliced along the edge. The blade cut through adhesive and paint layers. As he finished each side of the panel, he pulled the molding free and dropped it on the cobblestone patio.

Once he exposed all four sides of the square

panel, he pulled the screwdriver from his pocket. He pressed the flat blade between panel and frame like a lever and jimmied. The panel broke free.

Almost there.

He set the panel on the cobblestone. Slipping the knife between his teeth once again, he bit down on the blade. His pulse knocked in his skull, jarred through his jaw. If his father had installed motion detectors in the last years, Alec didn't stand a chance.

It didn't matter. He couldn't back out now. He had to finish this. He had to make sure Laura and his son would be safe.

Holding his breath, he squeezed through the space. His hands landed on cold tile. He slithered his legs through behind. Crouching inside, he braced himself for the scream of an alarm, the growl of a dog.

Silence.

He rose to his feet. Shapes of elaborate weight machines, a treadmill and an exercise bike hulked around him. The chemical scent of a Jacuzzi tinged the air. Movement flashed in the corner of his eye. He spun, leading with his blade.

A mirror's reflection shone from the far wall. Nothing. He was alone.

He lowered the knife to his side. A staircase lined a far wall, stretching up to his father's bedroom suite. Straining to hear over the tattoo of his heart, he crossed the carpet and climbed the stairs.

The hall at the top of the steps was black with shadow. Alec reached out a hand. Running his fingers along a satin-papered wall, he felt his way to his father's bedroom door.

A crack of dim light seeped into the hall. Alec touched his fingertips to the mahogany door and pushed.

Dim light filtered through a long bank of window sheers. The wide shape of a bed hulked along the far wall. A satin comforter shimmered, its gleam curving over hills and puddling in valleys.

Ivan Stanislov was in bed.

When Alec was growing up, his father had always slept on the right side, closest to the window. He'd bet the old man hadn't changed.

He edged across the room. Plush carpet muffled his step. Gripping the knife, he sucked in shallow breaths.

He had to kill. He had no other choice.

Reaching the side of the bed, Alec looked down on his father's face. Silver hair threaded brown, sparkling like stars against the dark silk pillow. A silver mustache lined his upper lip. But other than the slow creep of gray, Ivan Stanislov looked the same. The same line-free cheeks stretched wide over high cheekbones. The same gentle hook shaped his nose. The same full lips rested in something close to a smile. Everything about his father's face looked so much the same.

So much like his own.

Revulsion crept up Alec's spine and shivered over his skin. He had to get this over. He had to make sure his family was safe.

He moved over the bed. Taking one last breath, he pinned his father's body to the mattress and clamped his forearm against his throat.

His father's eyes flared wide. His body tensed under the sheets, strong as wire. He fought to ram one arm to the side, out from under Alec's weight, struggling to break free.

Alec leaned on him with force. Ivan might have been overpowering when Alec was a kid, but no more. Now Alec was in the prime of life. And Ivan was no match. He stilled his thrashing and focused on Alec's face. His gray eyes narrowed, hardened.

Rage shook Alec. Memories ripped through him. The sound of screams, of a baseball bat hitting flesh. The scent of blood. His own crippling weakness when he had seen Sally's beaten face and believed for a moment she was Laura.

Hatred welled in him, flooding his heart,

swamping his mind, threatening to wash away all thought, all reason. He leaned harder on his arm, jamming it up under his father's chin, forcing his head back, exposing his throat. Silver stubble sparkled and bristled over white skin. Alec rested the tip of his blade against a tender spot below one ear.

All he had to do was draw the knife across the carotid artery, the trachea, the jugular, and it would be over. The threat. The danger. The hate. It would be flushed away in a current of blood. His father's legacy would end with Alec.

Movement stirred on the edge of his vision. He glanced to the side. Bare skin topped one of the swells in the comforter. Brunette hair rested barely visible on the dark satin pillow.

A woman.

His father wasn't alone in the bed. Of course he wasn't alone.

Heat flushed through Alec, followed by cold. He looked down at his father. At the blade resting against the stubbled neck. He had to go through with this. He had to kill the bastard, whether he was alone in the bed or not. Alec had no choice. His father's legacy had to be severed. His unborn son had to be spared. Laura had to be safe. He could ensure all those things. All he had to do was press down on the blade. Slit his father's throat. Don't think. Don't feel. Be as cold as him. As brutal.

Just do it.

His palms sweated. His fingers trembled. The knife's handle grew slick as ice.

A distinctive click registered in the back of his mind. The sound of a hammer drawing back, a revolver's cylinder turning, rotating a bullet into place. "Drop the knife, Nika. Or I'll blow her head off."

The shape of a gun pressed up through the sheets. Its barrel pointed at the woman on the far side of the bed. He'd worked his hand partially free.

Alec looked down on his father's face, into the hard gray of his father's eyes. He had no clue who the woman was—wife, girlfriend, stranger, it didn't matter—Alec knew in his bones his father would shoot her. He'd pull the trigger and not think twice.

Red pulsed on the edges of Alec's vision, narrowing, closing. One moment of hesitation and he'd lost everything. Everything he loved. Everything that mattered. And now he'd lose his life. He pulled the blade from his father's neck and let it fall to the pillow.

Ivan's lips thinned into a malevolent smile. "Welcome home, son."

LAURA SAT in the passenger seat of Callahan's car, a little piece of her heart slipping away with each mile that hummed under the tires. He hadn't said two words to her. Instead, he'd ordered her into his car and spent most of the time they'd been driving muttering into his cell phone.

Laura had spent the time trying not to be sick. She felt so alone, so afraid, so confused. As if she didn't know anything anymore. As if she'd been caught in a strong current and was being swept along.

Laura cradled her belly in her arms. The baby shifted inside her, her abdomen stretching and bulging. She cupped him with her hand, caressing him through her flesh. Poor baby. He knew something was wrong yet was powerless to do anything about it.

Just the way she felt.

She turned to Callahan as he snapped his cell phone shut. His skull-like face looked even more drawn than usual, his thin lips even more bloodless.

She cleared her throat, willing her voice to function. "I need to know what's going on. Please. Tell me what's going to happen to Alec."

"If he is lucky enough to kill your father without being killed first, it's likely he won't make it out of the house."

"And if he does?"

"He'll be arrested for murder."

"Murder? What he's doing is self-defense."

"The threat has to be imminent for it to be self-defense."

"He tried to kill us. He's trying to take our baby. If Alec kills him, it's only to save our lives."

Callahan shook his head. "Not imminent."

"His men killed my partner and employees. They killed Wayne Bigelow and Tony Griggs. They shot a police detective. All to get to us. His men have chased us for days. How is that not imminent?"

"Your husband is trying to kill his father in his sleep. No jury in the country will be able to pretend a sleeping man is an imminent threat. If he succeeds, he'll be a murderer."

Breath whooshed from Laura's lungs as if she'd been punched. She doubled over, trying not to sob. Alec. A murderer. Caught in his father's web of violence. Everything he abhorred. "We have to do something. Something to stop him. Something to save him."

"I sent men to Ivan Stanislov's house to try to intercept him. If there's a way, they'll stop him."

She could only hope, pray they'd reach him in time. "And me? Where are you taking me?"

"To a safe house." He glanced at her. Dashboard lights glowed green, giving his face an eerie tone. His lips quirked upward at the corners, as if he was trying to smile. Trying to reassure her.

It didn't work. The only thing she could think of was Alec behind bars. Or dead.

Tears throbbed at the back of her eyes. A sob rose in her throat. She pressed her fingers to her lips, determined not to let it break free.

She couldn't give in. No matter what. She loved Alec. She wanted their little family to be together. What she'd told him in the motel room tonight was the truth. The only thing that had changed was now she was sure. Whatever he did, she would forgive him. She would trust him. She would love him. She wasn't going to lose her husband, her baby's father. She would do everything in her power to make sure of it.

Callahan slowed the car. Turning off the main road, he wound through a residential street. Green lawns stretched like golf courses in front of lavish mansions. Gardens of tulips splashed color over the spring landscape. Dawn's light pinked the sky beyond a giant Tudor of gray stone. Callahan swung the car through the open gate and onto the cobblestone driveway snaking toward the house.

A chill scuttled up Laura's spine and crawled over her flesh. "This is no safe house."

Callahan kept driving, one hand on the wheel,

his skull-like face grim. "I'm so sorry, Laura. I wanted to keep you out of this. I really did. But Ivan has given me no choice." He stopped the car and raised his hand.

In his fist was a gun.

Chapter Twenty

Ivan shoved the barrel of his revolver into Alec's face. "Are you ready to die, my son?"

Alec backed to the foot of the bed. Numbness settled into his chest and stilled his mind. He'd failed. He'd hesitated one second, two seconds too long. He'd allowed himself to think, to feel before cutting, before killing. And now it was all over. Now he would pay. He clenched his jaw. "You deserve to die."

"I haven't met a man who didn't." His father stared back at him, eyes flat as the dull color of slate. As if all the humanity had been bled out of him long ago.

"And women, too?"

Ivan glanced at the brunette.

Awake now, she sat up and backpedaled until pinned against the headboard. Whimpering, she clawed at the sheet, trying to pull it high enough to cover her bare breasts.

Ivan waved a hand in her direction. "Get dressed."

She slipped out of the bed. The dim light from the window catching skin, she scampered into the bathroom.

Ivan kept his attention riveted to Alec. Grabbing a red silk robe from beside the bed, he pulled it on. "We all do what we have to do, Nika. That's what being a man is about. That's why you are here right now, is it not? You felt you had to kill me?"

Alec gritted his teeth.

"Then you understand."

Understand him? The thought made him sick. "I'll never understand you."

"Maybe not. But it is not so hard. I am a man who does what needs to be done. A man who takes care of his own. Does that sound familiar?"

"I'm nothing like you."

Gray brows arched over dead eyes. "You're here. Pressing a knife to my throat, wanting to murder me in cold blood."

"I'm here to protect my wife."

"And your child. A son." His lips curved.

Rage overcame numbness, sweeping over Alec like fire.

His father's smile grew, teeth shining white in the darkness. "Don't you think I killed to protect you when you were a boy, Nika? To protect your mother? I did. I can't tell you how many times."

Alec turned his head away. Looking into his father's face, his father's eyes, was more than he could take. Bile rose in his throat.

"You still do not understand? Let me explain it to you. I grew up poor. Not poor like in this country. Really poor. I had to do whatever I could to survive." He stepped toward the wall and hit an intercom call button. "I decided as a young man that my son would never live like that. Look around you. The house, the businesses. I built this for you. I did what I needed to provide for my son. To make sure you had a better life."

"I'm not taking responsibility for the things you've done."

"There is a saying in Russia, 'The house is burning and the clock is ticking.' You do whatever you must to survive and prosper. Every day. Every moment. If that means steal, you steal. If that means kill, you kill. When you left here, you were too young to know that pressure. The pressure to survive. You know it now, don't you Nika?"

He knew it now, all right. His father had seen to it.

"But you failed, didn't you? Tonight you

failed. And in that, you are not like me. If it had been me with that knife, I would have done whatever it took to survive. I would have slit my father's throat and cut out his heart."

A thump sounded on the door. It flew wide.

Standing in the mouth of the hallway, looking at him with wide brown eyes was Laura.

No, no, no. Pain pierced Alec's heart. Paralyzing. Debilitating. Laura couldn't be here. Not here. Not in the same room as his father.

Callahan stepped up behind her, his thin frame towering over her in the doorway. "Stay right there or she's dead."

Alec glanced at the gun in Callahan's hand. A gun pointing at Laura's back. Hopelessness washed over him. When it came down to trusting a cop, he'd picked the wrong one. "So what happened, Callahan? Did Bigelow cut you in on this sweet little deal in exchange for help with his book?"

Callahan didn't answer.

His father's chuckle rasped from behind him. "The reporter? He was nothing. A nuisance."

Alec angled his body so he could see his father and Callahan at the same time. "Bigelow didn't tell you where we were? He wasn't on your payroll?"

"No. He asked too many questions. That's why he died."

Alec didn't need anymore explanation. He could put the pieces together himself. He'd asked Bigelow to contact the FBI, to request their help. And each time Bigelow had, Callahan had taken the information straight to Ivan.

Regret tasted bitter on Alec's tongue. Here he had doubted Bigelow, he'd believed his friend had betrayed him, when it was Callahan all along. No doubt he'd even manipulated the FBI guard at the motel in order to give his father's thugs the chance to display Bigelow's body. "Why, Callahan?"

The FBI agent's pale lips thinned. "It was you or me. Your family or mine. I chose mine."

Despair cramped Alec's neck and made his head throb. Maybe Callahan was a victim, too. Maybe they were all victims to his father's self-absorbed evil. He focused on Laura.

The same fear that chilled his heart shone from her eyes. But there was something else, too. Determination. Defiance.

It slammed him between the eyes with the force of a well-aimed bullet. Laura wasn't giving in to despair. Laura wasn't giving up. And damn it, he wasn't, either.

He set his jaw. He didn't know what the hell he was going to do to get them out of this mess. All he knew was that he couldn't give up. Not while Laura's life was on the line. Not while his son was in danger.

He *would* do what he needed to do.

His father ran a finger along the barrel of his revolver. "The clock was ticking, Nika. You should have listened. You should have slit my throat while you had the chance. Now all this is for my grandson. And I will see to it *he* grows into a man."

Laura raised her chin. Hands balled into fists by her sides. "You're no kind of man. You're a monster."

"Charming." Ivan punched the intercom button again. "Pavel? Where the hell are you? Get in here."

Another thug. No doubt Sergei wouldn't be far behind. Dread hardened in Alec's gut. It clogged his throat. He couldn't let this go any further. He had to end this now.

He met Laura's eyes, willing her to read his thoughts, willing her to understand. "Are you okay?" He quickly dropped his gaze to the floor.

Her lips pursed with understanding. Determination. Giving a groan, she buckled, falling to her knees.

Callahan lurched forward, trying to catch her, stop her fall. His gun tilted down, the barrel pointing at the floor.

Alec lunged at him. He struck his gun arm first, knocking him off balance.

Callahan held the gun.

A shot fired from behind.

Callahan grunted. Blood bloomed through his jacket sleeve, inches from Alec's face.

Alec jabbed his elbow into Callahan's face, hitting as hard as he could. He slammed Callahan's arm against the floor. He had to knock the gun loose. He had to stop his father.

Ivan moved toward them, his revolver in his fist. He reached for Laura, trying to get a grip on her hair.

She kicked, connecting with his knee.

Ivan grunted. Curses spewed rough from his lips.

Alec pried at Callahan's fingers. Using the side of his head as a battering ram, he slammed against Callahan's wounded arm.

The FBI agent still gripped the gun. He wouldn't let go.

Ivan grabbed at Laura again, catching her hair.

She screamed, the sound born from fury, not pain. She punched at his arm, at his groin.

He lowered his gun, pointing at her.

Fury exploded in Alec's skull. He wouldn't let his father touch Laura. He wouldn't let him hurt her.

He grasped Callahan's gun hand. He raised the FBI agent's arm, pointing the weapon at his father. Jamming his finger on top of Callahan's he squeezed the trigger.

Pop, pop, pop.

Shots rang in his ears.

His father stumbled forward. Toward Laura.

Alec shot again, hitting him from the side.

He hit the wall. His body crumpled to the floor. Blood blended with the silk of his robe, glistening red on red.

Laura lay next to him, her legs pinned under his body.

"Laura!" Alec tried to reach her. He had to make sure she was okay. She had to be okay.

She raised herself to a sitting position, his father's revolver in her hand. "I'm okay."

"Thank God. Is he dead?"

"I think so. I think so." She reached toward him, feeling for a pulse. She drew her hand away, fingers bloody. "He's dead."

Beneath Alec, Callahan groaned. His fingers went limp. Alec pried the gun from his hand. Standing, he crossed the room to where Laura lay. Using his foot, he shoved his father's body off her legs.

"Is he dead?"

The light Russian accent ripped through Alec

like a powerful electric current. He spun to face
the door and trained Callahan's handgun on a
young thug wearing wire-rimmed glasses. The
thug cradled an automatic rifle in his hands.

Alec kept the gun on him. Still crouched on the
floor, Laura did the same. But two handguns
would be no match for an automatic weapon. And
if there were any other thugs in the house—like
Sergei Komorov—the odds would be worse still.

Alec tensed, ready to throw his body in front
of Laura. To stop the bullets before they reached
her or the baby.

"Is Ivan dead?" the thug repeated.

"Yes."

A smile flitted over the hard young face.
"Good."

Alec narrowed his eyes. Had he heard him
right? Was this the thug his father had been trying to call on the intercom? Had he ignored the
call on purpose? What was this guy's game?
"Where's Sergei?"

"Dead."

"You killed him?"

"Ivan. Last night."

Laura sucked in a gasp. "Why would *he* kill
him?"

"Didn't ask." He looked down at Alec's father,
then back to Alec. "This is my organization now.

Understand? I improved it. Brought it into the modern world. I'm not handing it over to anyone."

Is that what this guy was after? The organization, as he called it? Was he looking to fill the power void now that Alec's father was dead? "I don't want it. Any of it."

"Good. That changes, and you'll be seeing me again."

"Then I'll never see you again. I can promise you that."

"Good. Go ahead and call the cops." He tossed a cell phone toward them. It bounced on the plush carpet. "The sooner they get this cleaned up, the sooner I can get back to work. I will be gone before they get here." Lowering his gun, he turned and walked from the room.

Relief nearly buckled Alec's knees. He reached for Laura, helping her up and gathering her into his arms. "It's over. It's really over." He kept the gun focused on Callahan.

The FBI agent groaned, holding his arm, but he didn't move.

Laura clung to him, tears streaming down her cheeks. "I love you, Alec. I forgive you. I trust you. I was worried I'd never get to say that to you, that you'd never know."

"Laura, I love you so much. I thought I failed you. I wanted to kill him so badly, to make sure you'd be safe. That the baby would be safe. And when I hesitated—"

"You couldn't kill him because you're not a murderer. You're not like him. You never were."

She was right. He wasn't like his father.

He'd worked most of his life to be different. To stand up to hate and brutality. To break away from that legacy of violence and crime. To not let it pull him back. And damn if he hadn't succeeded. And he'd succeeded in protecting his son from that fate, too.

But he hadn't achieved either alone. "You made me the man I am, Laura."

She looked at him, love shining from her eyes, a smile curving her lips. "No, you did that yourself. I just love you for it."

He slipped an arm around her shoulder and pulled her close. Warmth washed over him in waves. He'd been wrong. So wrong. It wasn't all over. The rest of his life was just beginning. A life of love and happiness and family with the bravest woman in the world by his side.

Alec flipped the cell phone open. And as Laura held the revolver on Callahan, Alec punched 911.

Epilogue

Dana Banfield braced herself as her muscles started to seize. The cramp pressed hard and low, starting in her back, then spreading around either side until it met in her abdomen. She cupped her belly with one arm, and breathed in and out through her lips until the contraction let up.

Next to her, her husband checked his watch. "That was less than five minutes."

Catching her breath, she nodded. "I think we'd better go. They say the second baby can come pretty quick."

Alec pulled her suitcase from where it was tucked in the closet near the door of their town house. No, not Alec, *James,* she reminded herself. She still couldn't get used to their new names. To her, they would always be Alec and Laura Martin, even though their lives had changed so much since those days—so much for the better.

After they'd escaped Ivan Stanislov's house that day, they'd decided to start a new life with new names and a new home near San Francisco. Although the young thug had promised to leave them alone, neither of them were crazy enough to trust a member of the Russian mob.

"Have you called Mrs. Jacobs?"

"I called when your contractions were still ten minutes apart, just to be safe. She should be here any moment."

Dana grinned up at James. She was so lucky to have him in her life. He really was the perfect husband. Protective. Caring. And as for the rest, time had made up for any differences between them. She supposed once you face death and loss head-on, what was important in life became a little clearer. Trust. Love. And family. "I want to say goodbye to Christopher. Explain where I'm going before she gets here."

"Good idea. Once she walks in the door, I'm sure he'll be so excited, he'll forget all about us. I guess Mrs. Jacobs is a lot more exciting than his boring old parents."

Dana couldn't help but smile. She grasped James's hand. Together they climbed the stairs and peeked into their son's room.

He sat on the floor, his legs folded under him, head low to the floor. Skyscrapers of multicolored blocks rose in front of him. Making a loud engine noise deep in his throat, he pushed a collection of trucks and cars, threading them over bridges and through tunnels.

James wrapped his arm around her shoulders. Warmth wound its way through Dana's bloodstream. After all they'd been through, they finally had it all. A marriage full of trust and love. A carefree three-year-old, whose life revolved around Hot Wheels and building blocks. And a little girl on the way. A girl she would name Sally.

Another cramp seized her. She grasped James's hand. As long as he was with her, the pain would pass. And then they would hug their little boy and drive to the hospital to welcome little Sally into the world. Together.

 HARLEQUIN®

INTRIGUE

The mantle of mystery beckons you to enter the...

MISTS OF FERNHAVEN

Remote and shrouded in secrecy—our new
ECLIPSE trilogy by three of your favorite
Harlequin Intrigue authors will have you
shivering with fear and...the delightful,
sensually charged atmosphere of the
deep forest. Do you dare to enter?

WHEN TWILIGHT COMES
B.J. DANIELS
October 2005

THE EDGE OF ETERNITY
AMANDA STEVENS
November 2005

THE AMULET
JOANNA WAYNE
December 2005

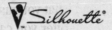

SPECIAL EDITION™

presents

the first book in a heartwarming
new series by

Kristin Hardy

Because there's
no place like home
for the holidays…

WHERE THERE'S SMOKE
(November 2005, SE#1720)

Sloane Hillyard took a very personal interest in her
work inventing fire safety equipment—after all, her
firefighter brother had died in the line of duty. And
when Boston fire captain Nick Trask signed up to
test her inventions, things got even more personal…
their mutual attraction set off alarms. But could
Sloane trust her heart to a man who risked his
life and limb day in and day out?

Available November 2005 at your favorite retail outlet.

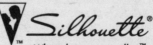

Where love comes alive™

If you enjoyed what you just read,
then we've got an offer you can't resist!

Take 2 bestselling
love stories FREE!

Plus get a FREE surprise gift!

Clip this page and mail it to Harlequin Reader Service®

IN U.S.A.	IN CANADA
3010 Walden Ave.	P.O. Box 609
P.O. Box 1867	Fort Erie, Ontario
Buffalo, N.Y. 14240-1867	L2A 5X3

YES! Please send me 2 free Harlequin Intrigue® novels and my free surprise gift. After receiving them, if I don't wish to receive anymore, I can return the shipping statement marked cancel. If I don't cancel, I will receive 4 brand-new novels each month, before they're available in stores! In the U.S.A., bill me at the bargain price of $4.24 plus 25¢ shipping and handling per book and applicable sales tax, if any*. In Canada, bill me at the bargain price of $4.99 plus 25¢ shipping and handling per book and applicable taxes**. That's the complete price and a savings of at least 10% off the cover prices—what a great deal! I understand that accepting the 2 free books and gift places me under no obligation ever to buy any books. I can always return a shipment and cancel at any time. Even if I never buy another book from Harlequin, the 2 free books and gift are mine to keep forever.

181 HDN DZ7N
381 HDN DZ7P

Name	(PLEASE PRINT)	
Address	Apt.#	
City	State/Prov.	Zip/Postal Code

Not valid to current Harlequin Intrigue® subscribers.

Want to try two free books from another series?
Call 1-800-873-8635 or visit www.morefreebooks.com.

* Terms and prices subject to change without notice. Sales tax applicable in N.Y.
** Canadian residents will be charged applicable provincial taxes and GST.
  All orders subject to approval. Offer limited to one per household.
  ® are registered trademarks owned and used by the trademark owner and or its licensee.

INT04R   ©2004 Harlequin Enterprises Limited

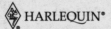 HARLEQUIN®

INTRIGUE

As the summer comes to a close, things really begin to heat up as Harlequin Intrigue presents...

Big Sky Bounty Hunters: No man's a match for these Montana tough guys...but a woman's another story.

Don't miss this brand-new series from some of your favorite authors!

Available at your favorite retail outlet.

www.eHarlequin.com

HIBSBH